AN AFFAIR TO REMEMBER!

Hi Akshatha

Here's

HAR eK KEE

RAT mein
ANAND.

LOV

Provir + Roopa
+ Mohit.

AN AFFAIR TO REMEMBER!

Harkeerat Anand

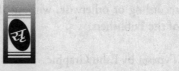

Srishti
PUBLISHERS & DISTRIBUTORS

SRISHTI PUBLISHERS & DISTRIBUTORS
N-16, C. R. Park
New Delhi 110 019
editorial@srishtipublishers.com

First published by
Srishti Publishers & Distributors in 2014

Typeset by Eshu Graphic

Printed and bound in India

Dedicated to the Munnis, Sheilas & Chamelis
of the world. May you be as infamous,
youthful & slippery (?) as you
are supposed to be.

*All stunts in this novel have been performed by
fictional characters, vastly superior to you.
Please do not try them at home.
Or go ahead and try them. I don't actually care.*

BOP. Forever & Beyond.

Before the madness begins

I would like to start by mentioning that I support the LGBT (Lesbian Gay Bisexual Transgender) community. You are nowhere in the story, nor have I ever had the pleasure of meeting one of you; I just think it is fantastic how you have gotten this whole acronym all to yourself. You also have that parade thing every year in a couple of cities. I like parades in general. And you have that failed actress give sound-bites for you, biannually, for whatever unfathomable reason. What's not to like?

If you are a person, animal, institution, thing or unidentified flying object who thinks this book is based on their life story, don't flatter yourself. Your petty useless existence has never managed to register with me; much less inspire me to write an entire book about you. In any case, my publisher has advised me to say: *All characters and organizations in this book are completely fictional and any resemblance to anyone – living, dead or comatose – is completely coincidental.* Even if it isn't, I am not going to admit it in writing.

Bad things happen to me. I have been stuck in three hour long traffic jams, suffered from food poisoning, had to work late nights only to watch someone else take the credit. I went through that phase in life where everyone gives entrance exams and prides in their meaningless ranks and percentiles and JEE scores.

I ought to be brain dead by now. But I am not. This information is of no help to you, of course, but if you have picked up this book in a bookstore (or worse, bought it), I guess you are beyond help anyway.

Passing thought… LGBT sounds like the name of a Delhi Metro station, doesn't it?

Next station… LGBT. Doors will open on your left.

Part One Begins

The first step towards sanity is to accept that you are insane.

Ogres, women & alcohol

"I... I... like you," he mumbled expertly.

I couldn't help but laugh. Ogre gave me a mean stare.

I took a sip from the thin red bottle, with gibberish printed on it, once I was done laughing. It was five hundred rupees a bottle (Ogre had picked it up from some pricey place), yet managed to taste the same as the cheap fifty buck liquor they serve at shady restaurants. Apparently it was some exotic foreign brand that *"had to be tasted to be believed"* (in Ogre's words, about two hours back). I kept grappling for some semblance of belief in every sip I took.

He put the phone down and looked at me sadly.

"What says this one, Og?" I asked.

He shook his head gloomily.

"So what does that make it?" I asked, picking up the sheet by my side.

"Two," he said.

"Three," I corrected him, checking out one more name. "You do realize," I continued, "that most likely you would be seeing these women again. And also possibly they might somehow talk to each other."

But Ogre was still in a world of his own. "What's happened to women, eh? How come everyone has a boyfriend? Or a career," he said, embellishing '*career*' with air quotes, "they want to focus on *right now*." He took a giant gulp of his beer. "You know what the funny part is? Every one of them and I mean *everyone* of them said- *I think we can be good friends though*."

"Why are you taking this personally, Og?" I asked. "You yourself said this is just an experiment."

He brightened up. "A *social* experiment," he corrected me snapping his fingers. "A social experiment," he repeated as if to convince himself. "Who's next?" he asked cheerfully, suddenly unmindful of the three consecutive rejections he had encountered in the last half hour.

Let me explain. The drunken social experiment had been inseminated by the birth, schooling and eventual college education of a nerd named Leonard Kinsky (The facts may be incorrect here or there because I came to know of them from Ogre himself, five beers down at that point. The experiment itself started a few more beers later.) So to continue... Kinsky was neither here nor there – not nerdish enough to be a Bill Gates/ Mark Zuckerberg and not manly/ soccer jock enough to not be called a nerd. Kinsky proceeded to Harvard where, as a mediocre mathematician, he made a startling discovery – getting a girl to go out with you was a simple matter of mathematics. Kinsky noted that the only thing preventing nerds from getting a girlfriend or in the short run, a date was being too afraid to ask women out or worse getting stuck on maybe a few or worst of all, one woman – a fallout of the "one true love" concept nerds are more liable to believe.

So Kinsky made a list of one hundred women and asked all of them out in a space of two weeks. Seventeen and I shall repeat in bold letters – SEVENTEEN of them – good looking to gorgeous, sentient, intelligent Harvard female creatures agreed to go out with this average looking short bespectacled mediocre mathematician. Kinsky's Love Law, also referred to as the Geek Sex Theorem and (though it was rejected by the Harvard Journal of Mathematics) also as the Laid List Hypothesis (when the story ran on a popular TV show in the US), proved that no matter how horrible you looked, no matter how nerdy, you still had a 17% chance of getting a hot girl to go out with you. Seventeen Percent. One in Six. For the worst looking nerd in the world.

Ogre looked, well, like an ogre. He was 6 feet tall at least... maybe 6' 5. His face was set in a hard strong bone/chin structure that made it seem as if he had probably just evolved, about ten minutes ago, from one of our Neanderthal fathers. He was neither the worst looking human nor a nerd; just someone who happened to be single and had come upon Kinsky's Love Law as an initiating idea and an innate exotic pricey beer induced courage to follow through on it.

"The next one's Radhika," I replied, a smile curling up at the corners of my lips. This was going to be fun.

"What! no no no no! No Radhika no no!" Ogre replied.

"Well you have to," I said, trying hard to conceal my smile, "Mathematics, Kinsky and desperate ogres do not discriminate."

"Asshole, she wasn't even on the list!" Ogre replied. "You put her there, didn't you?" He waved a wavering drunken accusatory finger in my general direction.

I smiled noncommittally. "Go on, call her up. We owe it to Kinsky," I said, raising my glass, saluting that horny nerd's satiated spirit in the sky.

Ogre muttered something under his breath that sounded like he was referring to my female relatives in the usual earthy manly fashion. "You do remember what she did on Karva Chauth, right?"

"No, Ogre, I do not know what she did on Karva Chauth," I replied truthfully. Did she perhaps offer food to one of the married fasting gals, resulting in the eventual complete/ partial destruction of the attached spouse, as in the legend?

"She kept the fast," Ogre replied simply.

"So?"

"So, she's single. Isn't it sort of desperate to fast on Karva Chauth if you are single, with no boyfriend or husband or fiancé or *good friend* or... or fuck buddy or whatever...

and with every male in sight steering clear of you?" Ogre replied.

"Which is exactly why you must call her, Og," I retorted. "Your run rate is worse than Kinsky's right now. Let's do Radhika just for the numbers."

I took a sip slowly and resumed, "Imagine that though, Og. This *pure pious* (Ogre smirked) gem of womanhood keeps a fast for the man of her dreams. And a month later, he calls her up, very drunk, and asks her out as a stupid prank."

Ogre, who had somehow become convinced quickly (perhaps owing to the significant volume of exotic beer now coursing languidly through his veins) and begun his search for Radhika's number on his mobile, waved me away.

But I persisted. "Oh! The mysterious ways in which the universe functions… What if the two of you got married? Went on to have kids?" I continued dreamily, even as Ogre dialled her number and put the mobile to his ear. "Aah the joy of watching a drunken mistake turn into a lifetime of pain."

"Hello Radhika?" he said. "Hi…"

I have no clue what happened next.

༄

When I woke up the next morning, there was an ogre in my head. You would think that with all the advances they have made today – science and stem cells and satellites that ensure you have Seinfeld on your TV and girls to talk to and ask out when drunk – as a social experiment, they would have come up with hangover free alcohol.

I kicked Ogre who had fallen asleep on the carpet, cuddling his beer. "Get up!" I shouted. He rolled over mumbling something incoherent, still cuddling the empty bottle.

I picked up the newspaper and the milk. They were setting up a committee to probe some scam; implicating someone in some scam; exonerating someone else of some scam. The entire first page was scams except the article at the bottom which talked of some drug that could boost female sex drive, which was most likely also a scam.

I heard a crashing sound. Ogre was up. "What day is it?" he said, squinting his half open eyes in my direction.

"Monday."

"Not again," he moaned. "I hate weekbegins." In Ogre's dictionary, *weekbegin* was Monday or whichever day the Week*end* ended. What can I say, he had a beautiful mind.

"Have they let off the minister yet?" he asked, rubbing his eyes.

"How did you know that?" I asked.

Ogre shrugged.

I went back to the newspaper, turning to the sports page. If the front page was scams, the last one was sex and infidelity

– Tiger Woods, Terry, Rooney. I managed to get one piece of real soccer news: Ferguson seemed to have given the hair dryer treatment (read as "flung a hair dryer at") to one of his midfielders, a recent acquisition from a little known second division club in France. I read on hoping that the hair dryer hadn't missed its target and given the French toad who couldn't string a pass to save his life, a decent sized bump on his head.

I browsed for about five more minutes before pushing off to the bathroom. I flicked the light on and started with staring sadly at my reflection, like I did every morning. A seemingly very old young man looked back into my eyes, in the mirror, like he did every morning. There were circles under his eyes and a couple of strands of white hair lurked in his sideburns. I was only twenty-six, yet could have passed for thirty, maybe more. I sighed and pushed myself to the shower. At least I didn't have wrinkles. Yet. Maybe I should start using one of those women's Age Miracle Creams, I thought.

It was only when I came back in to check the knot on my tie that I noticed it. To be honest, it was so faint that I wouldn't have seen it if I hadn't been focusing all my visual faculties on the knot. Just above my collar, on the left side of my chin was a faint purple bruise, about a centimeter in diameter. I ran a finger over it but it didn't hurt. Maybe I had hit myself while drinking last night. Maybe Ogre had punched me for making him call Radhika.

When I got out, I found that Ogre had gone back to sleep. "*Taking your car… Love*"- I scrawled on a post-it and stuck it to his forehead, smiling. One car for one bruise. Oh, Sweet Vengeance.

ABCDEF Corp.

When you are twenty-six (or somewhere in that age bracket) and still working for a software firm in India – your first job after leaving your engineering campus – you have very little choice but to do an MBA. You see people around you – people three or four years younger to you, MBAs all of them – earn thrice as much as you, get better sounding designations like a Junior Deputy Assistant Vice President (which sounds good although it halves "President" about four times) while you stay where you were four years ago, when the madness called your career began. Or perhaps get promoted a grade or two at best, with cosmetic increases in salary indexed to the inflation rate, not in India but Japan.

It ceases to matter that your firm is called 'ABCDEF Corporation' and that it is every engineering student's dream to land a job at ABCDEF Corp. That its share trades on the stock markets and is considered a bluechip and an outperformer and a heavyweight. That there is a grossly misleading advertisement doing the rounds on TV showing an employee from ABCDEF Corp. (wearing a cap or a jacket or a tie saying "ABCDEF Corporation" in font 120) solving the world's problems with software and technological innovations *only* ABCDEF Corp. is capable of. It ceases to matter that if you do an MBA, your career would look like the zig zag bowel movement of a fatally constipated creature – chemical engineer to software firm employee to MBA to consult/ bank/ marketing/ random employee at random company recruiting from random B-School paying big bucks and anointing you with a big title. All that occupies your mind is "God! I *have* to get out of here!"

But then B-school admission season comes and goes every year. You fill all the forms, dispatch all the demand drafts, pencil all those circles on answer sheets with your HB Lead pencil you once used to do sketches with and then settle into a wait. Trawl those chatrooms, google for answer keys from coaching institutes or for rumoured cut offs. You subscribe to *The Hindu* and *The Economic Times* and even religiously read them for a week or two before the results are out. And then you hang your head in disappointment, terminate your subscriptions of the boring newspapers (and go back to reading *Bombay Times*/ James Hadley Chase novels) and trudge back to the life you thought you were leaving behind. To become a President halved four times.

By the fourth year of giving CAT, XAT, FMS, etc., you are desperate enough to fill all the forms. You begin to "*dare to think beyond the IIMs*", toy with the idea of GMAT.

And then you are caught unawares. You realize that the B-school admission committees collectively believe that the stupidity/ inanity of staying employed for four years with ABCDEF Corp. has imbibed certain values, characteristics and experiences in you. And thus though your percentiles and percentages are much lower than your career highs, you start getting calls from the very B- Schools which are every disgruntled long suffering software firm employee's wet dream. You draft a *"Fuck you all! I am out of this hellhole!"* email and save it in your drafts folder and glow with barely concealed joy every morning you see it. Hadley Chase goes back on the shelf. *The Hindu* and long boring editorials walk back into your life.

And that is how I found myself registering myself for group discussion and interview preparations at this coaching institute a month ago. And with a "Fuck you all!" email in my drafts folder on my office laptop.

৪০

Monday mornings, there is very little difference between an office and a funeral hall. You enter at 9:30 and everything is deathly quiet except for the tip-tap-tip of fingers on keyboards.

At software firms, the sole differentiator to this communal funeral hall is an atmosphere of enforced excitement. There are balloons stuck to a few corners; a few buntings cling to a few walls, like creepy vines clinging to an old abandoned ghost ridden house. There is or are one or more posters saying random stuff like "ASPIRE!" or "LEAD!" with a grossly inappropriate photo from the animal kingdom (For eg: "LEAD!" is paired with the picture of a yawning lion) and an exclamation mark to boot.

As I walked slowly to my desk, I pictured myself, as I had done several times before, telling old Voldy I was quitting. Whenever I had the temptation to stop reading the immensely boring editorials and random reading material, I was subjecting myself to these days for my upcoming GDs/ interviews, I would picture myself telling Voldy I was out of here and then his possible reactions. It was my favourite daydream.

I reached my desk and switched my desktop on. Among the first few emails that came in, one stood out- flagged URGENT and with its entire body in a large red font. "10. MY OFFICE. YOUR APPRAISAL! OVERDUE!"

Crap. Not this again.

I had just begun adding a few more expletives to my "Fuck you" email when I felt a soft tap on my shoulder.

"Heyloooooooo," a sugary female voice said.

Crap. Not her again. I would rather have ten appraisal discussions with Lord Voldemort, I thought, or even spend five more years in this hellhole than have another conversation with her.

She tapped again.

"Heeeellllloooo," she said a little more desperately this time.

I swivelled my chair around slowly, sighing inaudibly.

"Sooooo howie was your week endy?" Radhika asked me, giggling at the syrupy torment she had just subjected a few more words of the English language to. I saw that she was wearing a pink dress, the color of those antacid tablets.

"Good," I replied, hoping if I kept my side of the conversation short, it would expedite her meandering away.

"Weee went to this movie. You know the one with the dancy dancy," she said.

My three-year-old niece used the phrase 'dancy dancy'.

"Okay. Good," I replied curtly.

"I'm forgetting... What was the name of the movieeee? Hmmm..." she continued. And I swear she actually tapped her index finger on her temple to think, like a three-year-old would.

I just stared at her blankly.

"*Arre* don't just sit there staring at me! Tell me the name of the movie naaaaa..." she said.

I shrugged.

"Useless you are," she said merrily. "*Achha anyyyway*, why were you not taking my call on Saturday, mister? You should have come to the movieeee naaaaa."

I shrugged again.

"Is there something wrong? Why are you not talking to me?" she asked, a few worry lines etching across her forehead, making her look like a particularly odd antacid tablet.

I sighed. "Look... I have my appraisal with RK very soon. Can we talk later?"

"Oooooh... so our Bond is worried about his appraisal," she said smiling. "Don't worry... *achha hee hoga*," she said, patting me on the shoulder with her left hand a few times.

I looked at my watch. It was five minutes to ten. "I have to go now," I said, getting up.

"Okie byieeeee. Lets catch up at lunch," she said, still giggling like a demented seven-year-old holding on to some secret. "Byeeeee," she said, before turning to walk away.

"Oh wait!" she turned back. "Tell me naaaa... do I look fat in this?"

That eternal feminine question!

∞

RK aka Lord Voldemort was not in when I walked up to his cabin. He had just gotten promoted a few months ago, largely – in my mind – on the back of the work I had been doing for him. Promotion meant a cabin, company car, a bigger sounding title, a fatter salary. I sat in his room feeling hopeless and desolate; I had gotten Rs 541 as my last performance linked bonus and had watched in amusement as the HR dude gave me a borderline funny reason for not getting promoted. '*You are not being promoted because no one from your batch is being promoted.*'

As I sat in the comfortable sofa that the Dark Lord's cabin afforded me, I wondered about several things. I wondered how and why I had become friends with Radhika. Why that damn anorexic skull of a woman worried about being fat. Why she had come to assume that we were *best friends* just because I had helped her out with one of her codes. I wondered how long the damn recession was going to last and ensure that I got peanuts for my annual bonus while the Dark Lord moved on to the better things in life a la cabins and chauffeur driven sedans.

I was just onto wondering which of the items in the office were RK's Horcruxes when he entered the room with a bang, having apparated from God only knows where.

He walked around his slightly congested cabin a couple of times before settling down in his huge imposing chair. I struggled to look uncomfortable and professional, nestled in the extremely comfortable sofa.

"So… appraisal… appraisal… appraisal," he said, tapping his fingers on the table. "Why don't you pull up a chair next to me, boy?" The damn man couldn't tolerate my being more comfortable than he was.

The reclines in both the currently non – RK infested chairs in the room – meant for guests and visitors to his lair – were quite broken. I was quite sure that old Voldy had broken them himself so that whoever else came to the room was always at unease while conversing with him. An evil but smart strategy.

I deposited myself on the less broken contraption and brought myself to sit next to him. RK was still drumming the table, occasionally muttering "Appraisal" as if it were some catchy song. Suddenly, as if inspired by an awakening inner demon, he arose from his reverie and picked up a paper and a pen.

"Listen, boy," he said. "I'm going to be very honest with you."

And then he began drawing on the paper what can only be described as a really complex geometry question in CAT.

A triangle came up first. It was then enclosed by a square, which eventually came to be engulfed by a circle. I wasn't surprised; I had seen this before.

He then begun shading in random places on the paper, inside and outside the weird geometrical contraption. I swear to God that he looked like a five-year-old doing his art homework while he did this. As the horrible looking masterpiece came to fruition, RK looked up at me with unsmiling eyes.

"Look boy," he began. "You're good. But you are only as good as the parts I have shaded on this sheet."

I looked at the paper with a little more interest this time. There was a lot of shading done in random parts of the sheet. The triangle was almost completely shaded but post that, everything was either shaded partially or less.

"You see here, boy," RK said, resting his evil chin over his evil fingers, his evil elbows on his table laden with possible

Horcruxes, "while you are pretty much doing your job, you are not going beyond. You are good, but you could be so much better. I see you going very far... in your career but you are your own enemy. You never take the initiative; never ask questions; never ask why this, why that."

I felt a fight rising in me. Bloody Voldy. Who was hands-down the best programmer in the office? Who was the first person he called as soon as he got a new project to execute? Who had slaved for him, making presentations late into weeknights and sometimes on weekends? Who had sacrificed sleep on the last project that had gotten him that promotion? Bloody fucking initiative... Who had volunteered to be Team Lead six months ago?

But as soon as I felt some *initiative* building in my fists I thought, "Fuck him". What was the point anyway? I had eleven B-school calls. I was bound to convert at least one of them. The statistics were against me staying on as Voldy's wronged minion for more than two months.

"As I was saying, I can't really rate you anything more than Satisfactory at this point... but you have six more months," RK said. "This is only the mid-year appraisal. Enough time for a course correction."

I just kept looking at the mish mash of geometry on his sheet.

"Boy?" RK continued, "You have anything to say?"

Yes. Go fuck yourself, I replied in my head.

"No. Nothing," I replied in reality.

He sighed. "Look boy. Nobody gets an *Outstanding* for just doing his job. You have to… have to go beyond," he said, his evil hands dramatizing a 'going beyond' gesture. "And further, it's recession time. Competition everywhere. You have to go even *farther* beyond," he concluded, hands in a 'going farther beyond' gesture.

"Look at me… When I was your age I was…" I switched off at this point. RK kept narrating some story I was sure I would have heard sometime in my four years with him… any one of those stories of how he made it BIG, he came to be my boss, came to be the Dark Lord. I yawned a couple of times to show my lack of interest in his evil past, gave the wall clock behind him a couple of sustained stares but RK was in his element. He went from one apparently inspiring anecdote to the other, unmindful that no one was really listening to him but himself.

I had just begun to wonder if there was such a thing as death by boredom when RK stopped speaking. "Good times," he said, looking nostalgic.

Before he could speak again, I stood up. "Boss, I have to go… meeting," I said softly, looking down at my watch for effect.

"Oh yes… work," he said, his train of thought quite clearly derailed. He was silent for five seconds before he began parroting, "Work work work… work." Another five second pause. "Good then. Nice session. *Acchha* before you go, how's Pay-Day coming along?"

"Coming along good," I replied.

"We are meeting the deadline, right?" he asked.

"Yes," I lied. And then looking at my watch again, I said, "I really have to go. Thanks for the time." And before the Dark Lord could think of anything else to say, I turned around and left his lair.

&

There was no meeting although I should have been having one. The deadline was four weeks away and I was the Team Lead.

I sat on my chair, idly sipping coffee, feeling nonchalant and rebellious. Now that I had been certified a 'Satisfactory Employee', again, I decided to act like one. I decided to spend the next few hours reading my boring editorials in the office canteen, not doing any work.

I got up and began to take out my stash of reading material from my bag. As I pulled *The Hindu* out, a small white piece of paper, a fragment from some page in a notebook, freed itself and fluttered down to the floor.

It came to rest on the floor, the pretty looping handwriting on it facing upwards, the words on it making me more agitated than Radhika or Voldemort or ABCDEF Corp. I picked up the damn fragment, rolled it into a ball and shoved it into my pocket.

Chemistry

Did you know that the same chemical that is used in paint lacquers is used for skin exfoliation treatments? Did you know that the only way to dilute sulfuric acid is to pour it on ice, as its reaction with water can cause a possible explosion? Did you know that a certain chemical used in automobile antifreeze is the poison of choice for several murderers due to its sweet taste?

I did not grow up wanting to be a chemical engineer. No self respecting human being grows up wanting to be a chemical engineer. Like millions of boys across India, all I wanted to be, growing up, was a cricketer. Or maybe a superhero.

Pages from Jain & Jain fluttered in front of me. Jain & Jain. That detestable chemical engineering bible. With its abstruse compounds and fearsome formulae and easy to forget facts.

As the dates of my interviews came closer into view, I re-ignited my torrid relationship with Jain & Jain, which had been gathering dust in a corner for about four-and-a-half years, being used as an indispensable cog in a three book foot-rest employed oftentimes whilst lounging on the bean bag watching TV. IIM Profs especially had been known to ask candidates disconcerting and unsettling questions from their graduation days. Though the general consensus among the people I had met (or taken advice regarding B-school interviews from) was to prepare/ mug up one "favourite subject", my desperation to get out of my pathetic I.T. company existence meant that I decided to subject myself to chemistry, in its entirety.

This added Jain & Jain to my seemingly ever-growing list of things to mug up; what with the world belting out one complicated Group Discussion worthy news item after the other. There was the Nuclear Deal which was not nearly as simple as its name, "1-2-3", sounded. There was the Budget which had ruined my life by outing a week ago. Then there was always some country or the other which would break out into some minor or major economic/ political/ social issue which would have to be read about. The Chechen rebellion in Russia; the beginnings of the sovereign breakdown in Greece; the plethora of realities that China was and still is. *The Hindu* was an adversary in itself because it was and has been, since time immemorial, the most boring, drab, colourless, dead and deathly serious newspaper – ever fearful of getting entertaining in the least bit. Even reports of Page 3 events in the Hindu's supplement would read like the election manifesto of some leftist party. I longed for my *Bombay Times* with its frothy news and colourful photos.

As time went by, the only thoughts in my head were a concoction of cumbersome chemistry, news items and random facts. I hated the editorials, I had always hated chemistry, but I hated Lord Voldemort and those irritatingly cheerful posters even more. There was a quiet niggling voice in my head that post MBA I was likely to end up in a similar situation – with a boss I would love to bash up and a company I couldn't wait to leave and a "Fuck you all" email on my laptop; but I shut the voice up thinking that I would at least be paid handsomely, whatever my future tribulations.

�❧

I had always been a great public speaker, so I wasn't really worried much about my performance in GDs and interviews; I had spent practically my entire school and college life on the stage. All I needed was the data; speech, I was convinced, would not be the issue. To sharpen my claws, however, I enrolled myself for practice Group Discussions at this coaching institute close to the office. 7 to 9 pm, every alternate day of the work-week.

A monitored Group Discussion is the most inefficient form of discussion, as I was to find out. I had only ever been in one GD earlier; the one that had gotten me selected to ABCDEF Corp.

The world had gotten much more complicated, vicious and dumb since and the stakes had obviously risen manifold.

In my first practice Group Discussion at the coaching institute, I couldn't get a word in for several minutes. Everyone was so charged up, so bloody eager, they forgot that this was just target practice, that the real deal was still some time away. The crowning point of the GD was when someone told me that my point of view was incorrect, when I hadn't really spoken a word at all till then. But the good thing, nay the great thing was, most of the people around me were so misinformed/ uninformed and yet so eager to speak nevertheless, they made incredibly ridiculous and terrifically enjoyable idiots of themselves. A voice in my head told me I needn't have worried. Just as the GD was about to close, I finally stepped in, told the bunch of idiots what the topic actually meant, what the difference was between monetary and fiscal policy and what "policy measures" were, with examples.

You know that thing that professional sports teams do before a big championship? Every year for example, prior to the start of the English Premier League Season, Manchester United will tour the world playing all these second string clubs, even college football teams and hammer them all 5-0, 7-0 and the like. Beat the minnows, get your confidence up and tweak the small things you need to tweak before the matches that actually matter, begin. Like Manchester

United, I had found my minnows. I couldn't have been happier.

I had spent a week (and 3 sessions) hammering the minnows, growing a little complacent even, maybe. At office, for the first time in my career, I refused to make this presentation the Dark Lord had asked me to make, much to his amazement. I felt limitless, invincible.

And then along came this girl. With unblinking eyes and unsmiling lips. That evil witch.

As the next week began, every time I rounded my voice to speak up at the end, she was there, with her unblinking stare and those lips that just would not smile. She had just joined our group that week – three sessions down the road – and for the first time, there was someone who actually knew her stuff, who could talk sense. And then, there were her eyes, her eyes from a horror story, staring at me as if they belonged to a snake poised to attack, her gaze seeping into my soul like acid; those lips incapable of expressing joy yet curling into a smirk at the corners, as if they knew whatever I was about to say was guaranteed to be stupid.

She took charge of the meandering discussions, drilled some sense, brought in some actual facts. She made my bursts at the end completely meaningless by nullifying the need for them... my confidence, which had hitherto been rising by the day, began to taper off.

I finally decided that this could no longer go on. The damn woman had ruined it all... I had to have my confidence and my stupid old minnows back. I decided to switch my schedule to Tuesday – Thursday – Saturday (from my current Monday – Wednesday – Friday). The bonehead who managed the administration at the coaching institute made some fuss before he let me switch. So that I could avoid her.

But she persisted. I had no idea why, but she happened to be there every day of the week. Even when (after a lot of haggling) I got myself shifted to the weekend only schedule. She was still there, day after day, 7 to 9. Eyes that didn't know how to blink, lips that didn't know how to smile.

Eventually, I gave up. I went up to the admin guy and told him I wanted out. He told me he was tired of me but there was no way the institute was going to refund me part or whole of the money I had paid them. He also asked me if I was mad.

With no option in sight, I decided to talk to her.

∞

It would be a few weeks before I could bring myself to finally confront her. All those days spent with the torture of having chemistry and appendages of pre-MBA interview material in my head.

I did a little bit of research. Her name was Ira Sharma. She was a final year student at some college – one of the ones that everybody seems to be proud of going to and for the rest of their worthless, meaningless, pitifully empty lives ends up calling themselves as XYZ-ians or XYZ-ites (whichever sounds more flashy) with XYZ being the name of the college (sometimes extended to schools too). She had also apparently done some part-time modelling but that, of course, is secondary to the plot.

Ira Sharma was obviously quite proud of going to the particular college. Close up, her face looked familiar, as if I had seen her somewhere before. She liked to describe herself as an XYZ-ian, which is an example of the fact that people from colleges like XYZ think they belong to a vastly superior species than us human beings. Us, poor humans graduating from nameless colleges, destined to slave all our lives for meagre pays for big companies that would give funny reasons for not promoting us.

I accosted her one evening, after the session ended.

"Look... I need this... please," I said, my hands folded together in a gesture of prayer.

"What?" she asked, confusion written on her face.

"I need... I need to be able to tell those guys they are stupid," I said simply.

She just looked at me wordlessly as if I was completely insane.

"See... before you were here, I had all these idiots in the palm of my hand," I said. "You... you have no idea how much I need them back. I need to be able to own them again; I need to be able to feel that confident again."

"So? What can I do about that?" she asked tersely.

I sighed, "Could you please take a break one or two days of the week? Or just shift to an earlier session a couple of days?"

She looked puzzled for a minute, but then an expression of lucidity came over her face. "Okay, whatever," she said. "Anything to get rid of you," she added, with venom.

I heaved a sigh of relief. I had been half expecting her to slap me.

"So, how will this work?" I asked.

"I will come in early a couple of days of the week," she said. "I'll SMS you the days, every week. Give me your number."

I searched my pockets, my bag. No mobile phone.

"You don't remember your number?" she asked, looking agitated.

I shook my head.

She gave me a poisonous look as she took out one of her notebooks from her bag which had '*XYZ-ian for life*' inscribed on it in an inclined running hand, large enough to be seen from miles away. "My mobile. SMS me yours," she said, handing me a piece of paper torn from her notebook. Her name and number in her irritatingly looping handwriting. A ten digit number, followed by "Ira Sharma".

Having handed me the piece of paper, she just turned abruptly and walked away.

I balled up the chit with Her Majesty's number and thrust it into my jeans' pocket.

When I got home, Ogre was sitting on the couch, surrounded by numerous six packs of what he claimed was a foreign beer that had to be tasted to be believed.

It was Sunday evening. The week was yet to begin. I was yet to be appraised as a "Satisfactory" employee; yet to meet Radhika in her indigestion tablet dress. Ogre was yet to get drunk and convince himself to call up women he knew and ask them out.

As I curled up on the couch, Ogre poured some alcohol on my arm and asked me if it felt cold. I jerked up in anger and threw a wild punch at him, but missed.

"Do you know," he said, "it felt cold because the alcohol was evaporating, having absorbed your body heat? Do you know, Mr. Chemical Engineer, that evaporation is an endothermic reaction?"

The Sedan

Most people would think that all you need to create an explosion is set a fuse to something inflammable and set it afire. You (being 'most people') will thus perhaps be surprised to know that you could drop a lit matchstick into a sea of oil and it will neither ignite nor explode.

Almost every explosive device will have a complex and precise mix of an oxidizer, a stabilizer and (only then) the actual explosive chemical, followed by a detonator circuit. The whole point of an explosive device is that it should explode on demand and not at its own sweet mercy, which is where the detonator comes in. Once activated, the detonator will send an electric shock wave through the explosive material at a speed of up to eight kilometres per second. The shock front, in turn, is what releases the immense amount of potential energy stored in the explosive. In other words, *boom*!

Lord Voldemort had no appreciation for the beauty of the complexity of an explosion. All that majestic intricacy fitted into a split second before the big bang. He just sat on his throne, pale and deathly silent, breathing heavily.

The catharsis of energy associated with even the crudest bombs made at home by terrorists has been known to create temperatures of a thousand degrees Celsius and their own shock-waves with pressures to the tune of a few hundred atmospheres. That's a few hundred times the pressure that your body can take. Not surprisingly, explosive shock-waves kill more people and cause more damage than the heat of the explosion itself. Imagine yourself getting crushed under the boot of an almighty giant, that's what a shock-wave will do to you.

The shock-wave is a beautiful and effective afterthought of the explosion. The high temperature at the epicentre of the blast will cause gases (generated in the blast) to move outward radially in a thin, dense shell that's called "the hydrodynamic front". This front then acts like a piston that pushes against and compresses the media of gases it encounters in the surrounding air, to make a spherically expanding wave of superheated gases, i.e. a shock-wave. And all this, everything, start to finish – detonation to explosion to shrapnel dispensation and shock-wave – happens in the fraction of a second, blink of an eye.

The Dark Lord still did not look impressed although that had never been my intention. All I had been trying to do was to make conversation with him. He just sat stiff and still in his chair, apparently incapable of speech, thought and cognition. And even though he was still the vile old Dark Lord, it was a little difficult not to feel sorry for him.

RK did not react as I got up and walked up to the cracked glass window of his cabin. Four floors below, RK's sedan was now a mangled post-explosion carcass, still smoldering and smoking – its roof gone, its seats and tires afire. There were three or four policemen scattered around the vehicle watching it burn, chatting with the security guard, sipping tea from plastic cups. It was entirely a matter of luck that the explosion had occurred at 9:30 in the night, when everyone (except the Dark Lord, the solitary security guard that ABCDEF Corp. employed and me) had left office. There were only a couple of other vehicles in the office parking lot, one of them my bike (from the looks of it, thankfully undamaged). No one had been hurt except RK's sedan, which had been totally annihilated as had glass windows of the floors closer to the ground.

I heard a knock at the door. A policeman in plain clothes entered and introduced himself as SI something.

He sat down opposite RK. I remained standing by the window, behind RK, facing the cop now.

"Sir, was that your car?" the SI asked RK softly in Hindi.

After a lag of about ten seconds, RK nodded subtly.

"Were you the one who called us?" the cop asked in English now, seating himself in a chair opposite RK, his English with a Marathi tinge.

"I did," I replied, putting my hand up.

The cop's gaze shifted to me. "Can you tell me what happened?" he said, directing the question at me this time.

"Well we heard a loud explosion and I called you… that's pretty much it," I said.

"And… what were you doing at the time of the blast?" the cop asked me.

"We," I began, pointing at RK, "were having a discussion about something in this cabin, when the car exploded." It was a discussion about me taking a two week leave for my B-school interviews which RK was dead against. RK hadn't really taken the news that I was trying to get out of the company well. He had just begun to threaten me with withholding my release certificate and benefits when the explosion occurred.

"Did any of you two see any suspicious characters before or after the incident?"

I replied with a "No". So did RK.

"Okay, that will do for now," the cop said. "Prima facie, it looks like the CNG kit in the back of your car exploded," he said, looking at RK. "No reason to panic. Consider yourself lucky no one was hurt." And with that he got up abruptly and left.

RK sat in the same posture he had been sitting in for the past hour – since the explosion occurred – immobile and shell-shocked. I dithered in my mind on talking about my leave with him again and finally decided against it. Imparting one final parting look to the view from the window, the destroyed remains of the car cackling merrily in the throes of the dark night, I turned away and began to leave.

I walked up to face RK on the opposite side of his desk and said, "Boss... I'm tired. Let's discuss our thing later." And with that, I began to walk slowly backwards toward the door.

I was just about to turn the knob when RK said, "Wait!"

I released the door knob, and wronged minion though I was, waited obediently for the Dark Lord's orders.

His voice quivered slightly as he said, "Can... can you drop me home?"

౭

RK didn't come in to work the next day which was a welcome break. He kept texting me orders from home, though (SMSes to the tune of "I need you to prepare that presentation NOW!"), which I conveniently ignored.

The charred remains of RK's sedan remained in the parking lot circled by a crude assortment of bricks and stones, which I assumed was the Bombay Police's state-of-the-art method to cordon off an area. A constable with a lathi remained seated near the ruins, smoking a bidi and brandishing the lathi at whoever tried to get too close to what was left of the car.

Along with Shinde, the security guard, I remained in high demand through the day. I kept getting treated to snacks through the day for my version of the story. Two reporters visited and interviewed both me and Shinde; one of them even photographed me and promised me that the photo would appear in print. A policeman visited and got me to sign some statement which pretty much repeated what I had told the SI the previous day.

At 4 p.m., I collected my four member team into RK's cabin and after the thousandth rendition of the explosion story, told them that I was most likely going to be leaving soon and they would be on their own for the project. They were all good guys – I had been lucky to get some of the very best – and I knew that, though all of them were at least one year junior to me, they would be able to manage without me. Further, what we were doing wasn't exactly rocket science; it was a payroll solution for large companies that had been done to death by software firms.

I chose Sudeep – the most experienced among them – as acting Team Lead, subject to RK's approval, who was to take over on Pay-Day completely once I was gone. We frittered away time discussing among other things, movies and my preparation for the B-school interviews. Everybody was really kicked about RK's car getting destroyed and overjoyed about him not coming to work. We debated for some time if ABCDEF Corp. was going to give him a new sedan in the light of recent events.

At 5, I asked everyone to leave and go home. To my surprise, each and every one of them – even Richa, the only girl in the group – hugged me before they left and wished me luck. I promised them that we would have a real nice farewell party before I left. A voice in my head said *"If you left"*. But I ignored it.

After they had all left, I settled myself in RK's throne, putting my feet up on his table. I put my hands behind my head and closed my eyes. In that one moment, nothing existed – no Ogre, no RK, no B-school, no career, no Deputy Assistant Vice Presidents, no XYZ-ians for life, no Ira Sharma. I felt completely at peace. As wind blew in through the open cracked window of the cabin, I felt a little emotional, even nostalgic about the time I had spent here. I wasn't going to miss working for RK and ABCDEF Corp., I thought, but I was most certainly going to miss some people.

Rapid Eye Movement

I n all my life, I had never and still have not seen a woman so beautiful.

Even the sun stared at her wide-mouthed, a creation of God so beautiful, so joyous that there was little else to do. The wind played merrily with her, her hair, whispered secrets in her ears.

She was beautiful in a way women have forgotten to be – a radiance, an expression of joy, perfect and pristine, perhaps even prehistoric. She had the eyes of a Basilisk, terribly potent and powerful; even while the rest of her stayed staid, there was life in her eyes. They laughed, frolicked, danced, spun, committed mischief. At times they spoke words, her eyes, in a language I did not quite understand. These words, as real as everything else around me, floated energetically to worlds far far away. Like birds of a beautiful blissful blessed species. A species I did not quite know or understand but had happy memories of.

And then, as if completely by accident, our eyes met. I stared fearfully into those big Basilisk eyes; asked questions of them, for they were beautiful enough to know everything. They looked at me as if I were their latest prey, their latest entertainment, held me in a hold so hypnotic and spellbinding that I forgot anything else existed. And just when they had done magic on me that I had not known could be done in a chance fluttering of my gaze into her grasp, they let go of me.

I woke up with a jolt. I reached out instinctively for my bedside table. Something made of glass crashed to the floor. It took me a minute to realize that I had been asleep, that I was in my bed. The fan above me was making a constant whirring racket as it rotated slowly enough for me to make out all its individual blades. There was juvenile sunlight coming in through the window colouring everything that it could in a cough-syrupy orange. I had no clue if it was dawn or dusk. Or what day it was.

I got up and walked up to the window, dodging the shards of glass strewn around. There was a pigeon on the sill, quietly, calmly watching the proceedings below. There were a few kids on the street playing gully cricket, making a righteous racket. A bunch of women, housewives most likely, were haggling with a vegetable seller over prices. This guy on a stationary bike was honking incessantly for an unfathomable reason. A street dog was barking mercilessly at a car for an equally unfathomable reason; perhaps he found the sedan offensive to his sense of doghood or caninity or whatever the dog equivalent was. None of this loud jarring reality could however shake that dream from my eyes.

I felt completely sure that I had never met or seen that woman before. Or had I? In my dream, I had known her, I was sure. But now that I was awake, her face was a blur; her beauty, her eyes were mere words. But even as the last vestiges of that dreamy liquid condition lifted from my head and reality hit me with its venomous and vengeful fangs, I felt equally sure that it could not have been a dream.

It was a memory.

∞

There was still a lot of beer left. In fact the number of thin red bottles seemed to have gone up.

I opened one and drank almost the entire contents in one gulp. I had nearly sweated myself to dehydration in my sleep. The fans were still whirring with very little enthusiasm. I saw that the black contraption on the top of the fridge was calling it 110 Volts. No wonder.

I finished the rest of the bottle in another gulp and opened another one. This one I was going to savour.

Ogre was on the couch doing something on his laptop. I assumed he was trawling Facebook, checking out pictures of good looking women.

"What may I ask is a *Slut Walk*?" he asked.

I shrugged and offered, "Horny females out on a walk?"

"My dear friend, your lack of knowledge of the English language never ceases to amaze me. For one, the word *slut* is unisex," he replied seriously. "It is the word *nymph* that applies only to women."

"Insightful as that is, why are we having this conversation?" I asked, settling down on the bean bag opposite him.

Ogre took a few seconds before he replied. "Well, I have been invited to this walk thing by a few people... Is it like supposed to be a communal dating event?"

I shrugged again. I had no clue.

"In other news, Radhika's tagged you in a post," Ogre continued.

"What! Why?"

Ogre got up and handed the laptop over to me. "My initial estimate is that she likes you. I think you should ask her out," he said, giggling.

I smirked. To my dismay, I found that Ogre was not kidding. She had tagged me and a couple of other people in this really horribly written poem on *Friendship*. It started with a sugary/ mushy nursery rhyme feel and went on to have a really macabre ending for a poem supposed to be about friendship. The last few lines were:

Will you hold my hands
As I die in the sands?
As I bleed to death?
And take my last breath?'

"This is so bad; she should be euthanized," I said finally.

"Don't really care. I'm through with that girl," Ogre replied.

I remembered Kinsky suddenly. "Hey Og, by the way, what happened that night when you called her up to ask her out?" I asked.

Ogre sighed. "Well mate... I never really asked her out. I think so at least. As far as I can remember, she picked the phone up and I heard that crazy voice again... and that was enough. I think I just gave her some crap about how we were really good friends and that we should talk more often."

"You've certainly dodged a bullet, my good sire," I said.

Ogre didn't reply. He walked up to the fridge and opened a beer for himself.

"I agree with you though, what you said that day," I said. "Something's happened to women these days... something's happened to our set of people altogether."

Ogre just sipped his beer in silence.

"Remember childhood? When we had one channel on TV?" I said, a realization knocking at the fringes of my mind. "When we had cassettes and big bulky cassette players and not MP3 players or iPods? And when... when it rained, we went out and played and didn't stay in because we could get sick with viral or dengue or malaria or that chicken-gun disease," I said wistfully.

"Good old days. Chandrakanta and Duck Tales and Tailspin and Super Mario," Ogre replied.

"Thing is, my good Lord, I think we just stop being happy as we grow up, we stop making friends, we stop connecting with people. I can spend, well *you*, you can spend 500 bucks on a beer bottle," I said, taking one look at the bottle in my hand, inscriptions in some foreign language on its label leaping out at me, "and still not be entertained enough… while as kids, that 5 rupees bottle with that marble in it would have made our day. You know that feeling we had? That feeling we had when the bell rang on the last day before summer vacation… coming home that day sucking on an orange bar, shirt muddy and untucked… coming home and throwing the bag away on the bed…"

Ogre cleared his throat before replying "Your point being?"

"My point is… I am wrong. And you are too. Nothing has happened to women, nothing has happened to people… nothing that hasn't happened to us anyway," I said, this realization finally dawning on me like a blinding orb of light in my head. "*Life* happened to us. We grew up, became engineers, then employees and we just forgot how to be happy… how to make friends. Look at me! You are maybe the only friend I have… everybody else is just an acquaintance."

"Well that really makes me sad," Ogre replied. He had gotten up in the midst of my rant and started combing his hair by the mirror we had in the hall, a prominent middle partition beginning to emerge on his head.

"Going somewhere?" I inquired. I saw he was wearing jeans and that gaudy T-shirt he liked to think made him look like a stud.

"Yeah... um..." he began.

"What?"

"Never mind," he replied. "Don't think you're in the mood for this right now."

"Ogre, we can do this the easy way or the hard way," I said, getting up.

Ogre sighed again. "Well, one of these girls I asked out that night agreed to go out with me."

"What! Really? What? Wow! How? Who?" I exclaimed shell-shocked.

Ogre laughed.

"Well, there was this... this," he began hesitantly. "None of the girls we knew would agree... and then I found this girl I had no idea existed."

"Girl? What girl?" I asked.

"I just called up this girl and we got talking for what seems like hours... the alcohol certainly helped," Ogre said, winking at me.

"You've never met this woman?"

"Nope," Ogre said.

"And yet you asked her out?"

"Yup," Ogre replied.

"And she agreed to go out with you?"

"Yup," Ogre repeated.

"How... why?"

"That my friend," Ogre began, giving the half-empty thin red bottle in my hand half a spin, "is the magic of alcohol."

I realized I had never seen the bottle from this angle before. There was a weird symbol on the back of the bottle, something I hadn't noticed before. It looked oddly like one of those skulls you would usually see accompany the words "DANGER! 1000 VOLTS!" There were a few sentences below the symbol in whatever foreign language the people who brewed and bottled this concoction spoke.

"Anyway, where did you... how did you get this girl's number?"

"Well you were holding on to this..." Ogre began.

Something made of lead dropped into my heart.

"...this piece of paper from a notebook with a number on it... and I just thought *what the hell!*"

I gulped. "Ira... Ira Sharma?"

Ogre nodded and began spraying deodorant on his armpits.

Part Two Begins

Zombieland

A City Maximum

Bombay is one of the cruellest, most miserable cities in India; a city so laden with unfulfilled dreams on underslept brows, with reality conflicting with the ambitions of a million, with an evergreen silent brooding painful struggle of the teeming have-nots versus a handful of ultra-wealthy with people like me, neither have nor have-not, stuck watching the charade from the middle.

Every one or two years, Bombay sees a riot or a bomb blast. And then, once the blood has been shed, tears have begun to dry, wounds have been bandaged and started their transition to scars, once the carnage has paused, if only for a minute, people return. Back to streets, back to work, back to the roads, as if nothing ever happened; something the media never fails to call the indefatigable "*Spirit of Bombay*". What they fail to see is the desperation, the despondency of the men and women who have no choice but to get out of the safety of their homes to earn their daily bread. For if they do not work, be it bomb or flood or riot or terror attack, they cannot feed their families that night.

Bombay is like its many men... zombie-like and brutal and omniscient of the harsh truths of life. The only people who can tolerate Bombay and even come to love it are those who have been born and/ or bred there and maybe also those who have too much money to have ever seen its dark side, whose walls are too thick for them to have ever heard its muted sobs in the night. City of a million broken hearts, a million scars, a million crushed dreams. And yet, a city of ceaseless and futile hope.

But then on one day every year, Bombay is unmindful of its tragedies. As Ganesh Visarjan dawns on the metropolis, teeming armies of otherwise morose and moribund men converge on Bombay's streets, singing, dancing, holding up traffic. The city is a canvas of colour with various renditions of Ganesha idols being prayed to and paraded around. For one day, Bombay is not the scarred marred animal it has come to be.

I walked in one of the parades as it proceeded to immerse a rather fit looking Ganesha, donning exaggerated six pack abs, in the sea. The procession danced and sang along deliriously to outrageous prayer songs, most of which were rather ridiculous do-overs of raunchy item numbers... for example, "Ganesha kee Diwaani" (adapted rather crudely from "Sheila kee Jawaani"). Some of them threw colour up in the air and on people; others distributed sweets. I watched from the distance as they reached the sea and began to drown the six pack donning, gym frequenting, weights lifting Ganesha in the sea water. After the precarious task of drowning the gigantic idol without getting drowned themselves, the men turned back, still ecstatically buoyant over their achievement. They walked back home, still singing the ridiculously inappropriate prayer songs, to have feasts and sweets.

The next morning, there was the usual sadness in the air. Humidity pricked at my neck as I stepped out. The air was shrill with hopelessness and despondence. The same tired zombies greeted me as I started my journey to the office on my bike.

Their hope rested at the bottom of the sea bed, somewhere near Juhu beach.

∞

Now that I see it all clearly, I realize it started with that dream. That dream stuck to my head as musical as the pipes of Pan, as delicious as ambrosia, as invigorating as the fragrance of a garden of a thousand roses, transcending my senses. I had her vision several times over... each version of the dream the same, the power and intensity of feeling getting exponentially stronger every time. Where had I seen this woman? Why was I so irresistibly drawn to her?

And thus I began to compare everything around me to that dream, to that feeling. Reality was so much more drab in comparison, so much more staid... it was as if she meant something to me; a memory reaching out to me perhaps from a tragic love story in a past life. I felt as if a chunk of my heart had just been cut off. Waking up was like walking into a great wall of pain, of needless reality. What was the point of reality anymore? And for all her beauty, why did I keep forgetting what she looked like as soon as I woke up?

Everything was a confusing congealed mass of emotion in my head. I felt tired; like I was done... I didn't want to fight anymore. There was this cacophony in my head, this voice that kept saying to me, *Why are you doing this? Why are you working here? Why are you giving these interviews? Where does this end?*

I sorely missed the simplicity I had known as a child. Life had become so maddeningly confusing – too many engineers, too many MBAs, too many software firms, too much traffic, too many smartphones, too much Facebook. All I wanted was to walk home from school just once more, shirt untucked and muddy, sucking on an orange bar, kicking pebbles. And everyone around me was the same zombie that the damn city is a mass of, swallowing instead of savouring, running their way around the maze like brainless rats drawn towards a piece of cheese in a mousetrap.

The only thing that made sense was alcohol. It felt right to drink... I had grown to acquire a taste for Ogre's beer. I would sit on the window sill, drinking, and look down at the hopeless masses walk either to or from the railway station nearby; all their expressions the same, their faces laden with a thousand burdens. And up in the window sill, I felt alone, with a thousand burdens and only one beer in my hand to dissolve them all.

I felt completely lost, lonely. Unloved.

Ogre, on the other hand, seemed to be getting happier everyday with the love story I had unwittingly engineered. He laughed, hummed, smiled for no reason at all. And then told me stories of his last date. Of the last funny thing she had said. He seemed to be smitten.

Perpetually drunk, tired and depressed – unable to banish that dream and Ogre's happiness from my head, unable to make sense of why I was doing what I was doing – I stood at the precipice of detonation. Writhing in agony, waiting for someone, something, anything to light my fuse.

The slave, the pageant and the empire

Every few months, someone really senior usually thought it worth his while to embark on a visit to our office. These visits were akin to the visits of British emperors to the far flung fiefdoms they owned. And much like the theatrics of early twentieth century, when royalty was welcomed with parades of elephants, horses and associated pageantry and anthems written especially for them (Even the Indian National Anthem was originally written as a welcome song for King George V), the organization went to ridiculous extents to ensure that senior management thought that everything was happy and gay at large.

It seemed like a ruddy good job to me – travelling office to office on the company's dollar; putting up in five star hotels; receiving salutations from hundreds and thousands of slaves bent forty-five degrees in obeisance, chanting songs of your praises and offering rather exaggerated explanations of what pitifully little they did and how useful they were to the company; dining on company sponsored food (not that cheap tasteless detestable canteen stuff, but pizzas and pastas and maybe even alcohol); being hit on by both men and women alike, desperate for an opportunity to get inducted into royalty and receive salutations themselves; talking down in a booming voice to people desperately hanging on to your every word; using every opportunity you got to shake someone's hand and in effect, flash that really cool looking expensive watch, one of which you buy yourself every month. Life after MBA was good, I told myself.

Now that he knew I was most likely leaving, RK had been more torturous than usual. I had spent the last couple of days late in office, making presentations and spreadsheets he was supposed to show Mr. Senior Management (which, in retrospect, I should have been grateful for; the house had become a depressing hotbed of alcohol, visions and dark thoughts). In big companies like ours, presentations are essentially the preferred language of communication. What I could tell you in one crisp page of a Word document had to be spread out over twenty slides for Mr. Senior Management; slides packed with Smart-Art and Clip-Art and thought bubbles at the bottom and enough text to leave a normal human being brain dead from trying to comprehend the deluge of material.

Yet for all his evil hold over me, RK had failed to get me to shave. He had spent the best part of an hour giving me tips on personal hygiene, a couple of hours prior to Mr. Senior Management's descent in our ramparts. He had explained repeatedly how beards were not professional and even brandished an electric razor at me, one that he apparently carried in his laptop bag for "shaving emergencies" (whatever that meant and however they transpired in his evil little world). I stayed resolute, however, and much to the Dark Lord's chagrin, presented myself to Mr. Management unkempt and unshaved.

My mind slept through RK's presentation (or the presentation I had made); an event to which I think I was only invited, despite my facial hair worthy of a shaving emergency, because I was sure RK had just hurried through the contents of the presentations I had made on his way to office. Most likely, the useless slob hadn't even done that, and would have believed me useful in an emergency, in case he could not pronounce or understand a big word, for instance. At my end, I had used all my entrance exam preparation to fill up the presentation with really big sounding words, so that the presentation was as easy (or difficult) to read as an Alistair Maclean novel. (For those of you who haven't read Alistair Maclean, you cannot read one of his novels without consulting the dictionary at least once, every half sentence or less. You are an English professorial demi-god if you can go through one whole page without consulting a dictionary. I am pretty sure Mr. Maclean didn't have a splendid vocabulary at all; he just sat with a big Thesaurus by his side, inserting a big sounding word every four words in whatever military adventure nonsense he was writing about.)

To my amazement, RK had been tardier than I could have ever given him credit for being. He hadn't even deleted my comments from the excel sheets or presentations, meant for his eyes alone. Rather he read a couple of them out to the audience of Mr. Visiting King from far flung kingdom, a couple of the seniormost vassals in our own fiefdom: a Vice President (equivalent in grade to RK) and an Assistant Vice President in the Bombay office, and then me – a hirsute lowly prisoner with aftereffects of last night's foreign beer still ringing in his head.

I beamed secretly in barely concealed joy as the Dark Lord read a couple of my comments which said something to the tune of *"Numbers not adding up!"* and *"Consistent Mismatch"*. He went on to read a couple of slides verbatim. I was sure he did not understand the heavy words used therein. I had written RK a detailed email on where all the financial excels he had given me for processing and the data I myself had downloaded from the company intranet did not match. It was apparent now that he hadn't read my email at all and gone straight to the attachments. Mr. S. Management had an expression of slight disappointment on his face.

As Mr. S. Management scratched his chin, I finally recognized him. He was the CFO, I remembered, the Chief Financial Officer; he had given an hour long chat on *"A career at ABCDEF Corp."* (which more appropriately should have been titled *"Lack of a career at..."*) during our induction into the firm, four long torturous years ago. He had had a goatee then (which he would scratch whenever someone asked him a rather stupid question or gave a stupid answer), as also more and darker hair than he did now. He seemed to have aged horribly in just four years, making me doubt the luxury of the royal life for a fleeting second.

As RK bumbled on and the now goatee less chin of royalty was scratched more vigorously – in disappointment (I assumed) – to my left, I found my mind going back in time to those early induction days at ABCDEF Corp. Our initial few days and weeks of slavery, when we had been naive enough to believe that we could make good money and have a career here.

∞

We wore nametags.

"Hi. I am Swati. From Roorkee. "

Her nametag agrees.

"Hi Swati," you say automatically.

"Hi. I am Arun. I am from IIT Delhi". And the nametag tallies.

"Hi Arun," right hand automatically extended for handshake. Lips automatically curled into a fake smile.

"Hello. My name is Sumit."

"Hi Sumit."

"I am Radhika. Hiiiiiiiiiiii!"

There were so many of us that we had to wear nametags for the ringmasters to recognize us. And yet when we introduced ourselves to each other, we spoke out our names. Our very redundant pointless names, printed on nametags and pinned to our chests.

The very first day of ABCDEF Corp., there were introductions. I shook hands and forgot people's names. Employees who had already been slaving for ABCDEF Corp. for some time mingled with us without nametags and spoke politically correct fluff about working here. I feigned interest.

I gave them a name different from the one on my nametag. Somewhere, there was a Ryan in the room who was either roaming about without a nametag or was wearing mine. None of the names I gave or wore were real.

Hi. I am Ravi- I would say. Sometimes I was *Puneet*. Or *Kunal*. My nametag was Ryan all through.

No one seemed to notice. They all shook my hand and forgot my name. I was never really one for pranks but I was bored. And a little drunk on the cheap champagne they served at the orientation party. The party was a great grand illusion; it intended to say to us: *working here's one big party*.

We made polite and official dinner conversation. *Which college are you from? Oh, my friend's cousin's dog-walker's girlfriend's neighbour studies there. Perhaps you know him? No? Oh okay.*

No one else from my college got selected. I was unknown and friendless. I was Ryan and Ravi and Puneet and I was twenty-two and my girlfriend had just broken up with me a week ago. She had made it to an IIM and promptly switched her romantic interest. That bitch.

So I was twenty-two, girlfriendless, wearing the wrong nametag and very confused about what I was going to do with my life.

The hall was huge and showy; the hundred odd nametagged newbie slaves inside it had already started schmoozing with the nametag-less pre-enslaved. The human instinct of mindless ass kissing was at play and I watched it from a distance with a vodka cocktail in my hand.

His name on Facebook was *Ravi SuperAwesome Prasad*. And it said that he was in a relationship with her, the ex girlfriend. Also, he was from some IIT, loved working out, playing the guitar, watching F1. Both of them had the same Facebook photo: a vomitishly sweet picture of them standing staring into each other's eyes, holding hands. In a couple of years, they were going to make four times the money I made and cute little post-MBA babies.

I was drunk, depressed and quiet in a corner of the big showy hall. I knew she didn't dump me for the first guy she met at her IIM. We had been over for a long time. Only too afraid to accept it. I was nameless in a crowd of a hundred ass kissers and I pretended I was Ravi SuperAwesome Prasad, amongst other names. I played the guitar and loved working out. Then, I was Kunal who was a footballer and loved to write poetry. Puneet was a nerd who read Alistair Maclean novels and went pages without consulting a dictionary.

Yet, for all my pretenses, I felt no different.

I was drunk and depressed and quiet in a corner of my mind.

"You really shouldn't drink that much," someone said.

I turned my head to see a mountainously built man standing behind me. He did not wear a nametag.

"Why?" I asked instinctively.

"You have been swaying for some time now," he said smiling.

I turned completely, staggering drunkenly a little bit and offered him my hand "Hi. I am Ravi," I lied, "…and you?"

"I am Ryan," he said, smiling and pointing at the nametag pinned to my chest, "but they call me Ogre."

And that is how we met.

৪৩

The CFO's royal booming voice cut into my reverie.

"Is that all?" he said, pointing the question at RK. RK nodded a slight nervous nod.

RK had a weird expression on his face. I realized it was a mixture of relief, nervousness and his residual evil.

Mr. CFO politely pointed out the shoddiness of the presentations. I scratched my stubble, worthy of a shaving emergency, nervously hoping none of the fallout reached me.

It didn't. Not yet.

RK would give me a long lecture on how to make presentations for senior management the day after, though. I would listen with my ears shut and an expression of disdain on my face, much to his chagrin.

Presentation over, Mr. CFO and the senior vassals retired to another room for refreshments. Happily for me, I was excused.

I walked out of the conference room and knowing that RK was going to be tied up until Mr. Senior Management left late in the evening, I decided to head home.

As I walked out of the office building towards my bike, I realized it had been months, maybe years, since I had seen the afternoon sun on a weekday.

It felt good. In that one fleeting moment, I felt happiness filtering through to my heart like a ray of sunlight filtering through a thick dense layer of monsoon clouds.

There is life on Mars sometimes

Monday mornings were devoted to project update meetings.

This Monday morning, there was mathematics in my head. More and more, I had been having funny thoughts.

While giving RK a clueless expression and a nonchalant shrug in response to his question, I calculated that every minute I worked cost the ABCDEF Corp. a princely sum of three rupees. While that was not really much, it was heartening to know how it all could, potentially, add up.

That coffee break. Thirty bucks per head. Ask a couple of people to join you and you have successfully frittered away a hundred bucks of official time in ten minutes.

That informal Friday evening chat. Fifteen bucks per head.

Did Radhika look fat? Ten rupees per head.

Then one day you were late for office and you looked at the watch every thirty seconds. There was this 9 a.m. update meeting at work and your life was ending minute by minute in inexplicable unprecedented Bombay traffic. Breath by fucking breath; three bucks at a time.

RK was looking at me angrily, saying something which didn't register. His eyes were on my hair – my bed-head – half of my hair (the right half) were standing erect as a tower. The other half were sticking out, drunk as me, in different directions.

You were a damn speck on the face of the earth and someone, someone you had never met, had valued your life at three bucks a minute.

Inside my head, the calculator ran. Every twenty extra seconds spent at the urinal meant an extra rupee you merrily pissed away.

It wasn't much. But it all added up.

Of course, the more senior you got, the more valuable your piss was. RK's minute at the loo cost the company ten rupees.

The CFO's royal piss probably cost fifty bucks. Or more, considering he had all those perks, all those stock options. I heard a flush sound in my head; saw the CFO's nutrient rich big buck piss going round and round down the urinal drain.

There was conversation on around me. Sudeep took on some of the questions meant for me. Good man.

RK never read emails. Or listened in general. It didn't really matter what anyone told him because he would forget everything in approximately ten seconds. Have you seen those goldfish bowls? Goldfish have no Random Access Memory at all; they have a memory log of maybe about five seconds, post which everything gets wiped out. Which is why they circle around in their minute fish-bowl universes, happy and content, their five second amnesias kicking in continuously throughout the day.

I saw RK processing information. I imagined his brain whirring from the effort like one of those old overworked decade old desktop computers. *Beep. Beep. Whirrrrrr. Ten seconds and two rupees before brain shut down and reboot.*

A chimpanzee with a nicotine addiction and half addled brains could have done RK's job. All he ever did was collect information from us slaves in these meetings and pass off the work we did as his own.

But there were perks to this modus operandi. Just slip in one half true fact, just one lest the addled chimpanzee should realize you were up to something, and watch him make a fool of himself.

Thirty minutes of meeting. Five hundred and fifty rupees of collective time wastage.

Five hundred and fifty bucks of nutrient rich piss down the urinal drain. Round and round.

It all added up.

∛

Just as an experiment, I let one of them fall off my hand.

It fell, its angle staying true to me all along, the skull sign on its back getting progressively smaller with every passing microsecond. I looked at my watch and it was counting time in rupees. Every minute was three rupees. Every microsecond was zero point three paisa. Simple math.

My feet dangled off the wall and there was another one at the ready in my right hand, ready and willing to follow the first one to death by gravity. Time passed in paise, slowly, grudgingly.

Finally it crashed, breaking into a million pieces, but grudging and unwilling to reimburse me my paise as time was, all in slow motion. And then it knew peace. No more beer. No more water. Or being refilled. Or having some school kid grow a damn tree in your inside. Nothing but a million pieces of glass.

No more need for a career. No need to do an MBA.

Nothing but a million pieces of glass.

The skull printed on the other one looked at me and smiled. And said '*Please*'.

I stood up on the wall and bowed before the second empty beer bottle. Even the inanimate deserve ceremonies. The skull smiled back.

And then I tossed it in the air upwards. It made that parabola as it fell, as Newton's physics said it would, and then ever so slowly began to comet its way down to the earth. Skull smiling. Time grudging. Beer bottle willing.

In that one fleeting second before it kissed the ground and shattered into a gazillion pieces, the skull burned as if alight, warm and red, and then it was gone. Nothing but a million pieces of glass.

I stood up on the wall; I could hear the ground below me call out to me. It had tasted enough glass, not enough blood and bone.

I spread out my arms and closed my eyes. The wind rustled through my hair whispering *"Jump! Jump!"* in my ears. If I jumped, there would be nothing else; no more career, no more MBA, no more RK, no more Ira Sharma. That damn woman. Nothing but my skull twisted and contorted smiling up at the sky. Nothing but a million pieces of bone.

I opened my eyes and there she was again in front of me. Her smile burned as if alight, warm and red, singing a path through my chest. That wicked smile. That self content smile of contempt. Those lips incapable of expressing joy yet curling into that iniquitous old smile, as if they knew whatever I was capable of saying or doing was guaranteed to be stupid. The mysterious beauty of my dreams with eyes committing mischiefs and magics. And that hideous evil smile.

Describe yourself in fifty words or less: a random form belonging to random B-school said.

It also asked me my vision and mission statement. I had no clue what either word meant and what the fuck was the difference between the two.

The damnably beautiful woman of my dreams batted her eyelids at me again, magically majestically. But I was drunk and immune to her charms. My arms still spread out like giant wings, I looked down the wall. The ground below waited patiently for me to jump.

You grow up thinking that this one day I am going to be happy and done. You pass your boards, which your parents told you would make or break your life (*Not career, life!*), and you are not done yet. You then go on to do your engineering, thinking year after year, as you hate yourself for subjecting yourself to it, that once this bullshit is over, I will be done. Then engineering gets followed by a job. Job by MBA. MBA by EMIs for that education loan. And then you have that career you always wanted and a big sounding title and you want a bigger sounding one. A bigger car, a fatter EMI. You can never really ever be done.

Your empty life can never be described in fifty words or less.

What is your statement of purpose?

I stood at the precipice, completely void of a statement of purpose or a life that could be described at all, being stared at by big beautiful magical eyes, my wings spread wide. I stood there and wanted to be done.

Obituaries charge you by the word. I would jump and be done. And then somebody would describe me in fifty words or less. Probably much less because obituaries charge you by the word.

He was a gem of a person with a drinking problem, who had no mission or vision statement. He could have gone very far but he was his own enemy; he never took initiative, never asked questions, never asked why this, why that.

The light is gone from our lives. Blah blah blah.

He will be remembered by all.

Accompanied by a disturbingly happy looking passport size photo of me.

Death is not cowardice. Living is. So afraid of the inevitable, you keep on breathing, keep on living – rats in a race, hamsters on a wheel. Never happy. Never done.

If I jumped, I would finally be done. No more mission statements. No more career. No more haunting memories. Nothing but a million pieces of bone.

I drank in one last breath. *One last one and then I jump,* I told myself. And then cheeks stuffed with my last living breath, I jumped – headfirst, as if diving into some celestial swimming pool. Give or take a couple of microseconds to the effect of earth's atmosphere, I knew the exact amount of time I would take to hit the ground. But even as the countdown sounded in my head I fell slowly, gravity as if ceasing to exist, every passing second becoming heavier, more viscous, slowing me down as I fell. The eyes of the angelic beauty with the demonic smile followed my descent with interest.

And in that one last microsecond, in that smallest possible currency of time before I hit the ground, nothing really happened. My life didn't flash before my eyes. Nor did my most or least favourite memories. There was just a feeling of about to be done; happiness just about knocking at the door. That last microsecond could well have been an hour, such was the viscosity of time; the dullness of gravity that I felt as if I had been floating an inch above annihilation forever. As if no one – not time, not gravity, not that beautiful woman – wanted me to be happy and done.

But finally whoever or whatever force held me back let go and I fell.

I would shatter into a million pieces of blood and bone; a million tons of pain.

But I did not.

The ground caved in, letting me fall more, absorbing my kinetic energy like a sponge. And then the ground was water and instead of being in a million pieces, I was one whole piece drowning, unable to breathe, the reality above me refracting and shimmering in through the water's surface. Even as I flailed my arms and grasped for breath, I saw that evil witch's gaze, unrefracted, unshimmered, burning through the water's surface. My lungs began to burn with water I had involuntarily begun to swallow, my half addled brain mistaking it for oxygen. I was now at a stage where my brain had gone without oxygen for a sufficient amount of time, which if Reader's Digest is to be believed, would most definitively lead to some sort of impairment even if I were rescued, remote though the chances of rescue were.

The light is gone from our lives. He died a painful death squirming, struggling for oxygen, drowning in the very muck his life had come to be.

I stopped struggling and began to give up. My nostrils, throat, ears, all burned as if from severe acid reflux. Death was near. Finally. Thankfully.

And just as my sight began to leave me and my heart began to stop pumping blood, something pulled me up. Strong arms, big hands, belonging as if to some monster. With the monster's aid, I broke through the water's surface, gasping for breath. The monster sat me upright, waiting patiently for me to regain my senses.

I realized I was panting heavily and almost completely soaked. My eyelids refused to open. I tried to rub my eyes with my hands, which, shivering severely, kept missing their mark. Finally my brain chugged to life and began attempting to make some semblance of sense of the puzzle I had just lived through.

"You've been dreaming... for a rather long time," the monster said.

I looked up and saw the familiar face for ten whole seconds before recognizing it. Ogre.

"Glabaabaadoo," I muttered.

"What?" Ogre said.

I waited for a couple of more seconds for my brain's speech centre to activate.

"W... what hap... pened?" I realized the thing my clothes were soaked from was my own sweat.

Ogre looked at me, as if with pity, for a moment before he replied. "You know you really shouldn't drink this much."

I shrugged. "Is that why you woke me up?"

"Nope," he said. "Get up. You've got to see this."

"See what?"

Ogre gestured for me to get up and follow him.

I got up, my legs wobbling from the near death experience my foolish brain was telling them we had just had. I followed him to the common area of the house where every light was off except for the TV. It was one of the darkest nights I had seen in Bombay; the dark filtered in through the windows making the TV look like an odd beacon of hope amidst the gloom.

Ogre pointed wordlessly towards the TV where a really enthusiastic reporter was going at some piece of news with real gusto, touching his ear piece repeatedly, speaking a million words a minute and shifting from foot to foot, as if subconsciously dancing with barely concealed joy. I rubbed my eyes again and then my ears, because what he was saying had to be a joke. For one fraction of a second, I thought I was still in my oddly real dream; parts of it still played hauntingly in my head. But then I saw the expression on Ogre's face and realized I was not.

"…apparently an email from a junior employee dated the twentieth of this month began the end of the company," said the reporter, his subliminal joy at covering the story bursting through him. "In his letter of which our news channel has an exclusive copy, the CEO said it was like *quote-* riding a tiger not knowing how to get off its back without being eaten. *Unquote.*"

And as they dissected and autopsied the scam on screen, I realized that the '*email from a junior employee*' they were referring to was my email to RK containing the CFO's presentation.

Dawn of the Undead

The average life expectancy of a soldier in the Normandy Invasion during World War II was twenty-two minutes. If you were a poor sodden deathward bound bastard of a soldier in the Allied Army heading towards the French coast in an open navy boat on D Day – part of the first wave of invaders – the most mathematically logical thing you could be advised to do was to light up a cigarette, turn on your stopwatch, drag in long tobacco laden contented last breaths and prepare to be riddled with bullet holes in precisely twenty-two minutes. In the end, inevitably, mathematics would ensure you were dead.

The next day in office, the most mathematically logical thing to do was to light up a cigarette and watch the carnage unfold. Somewhere in the office, Ogre was having a meeting with whatever was left of our batch and a few others to *'Chalk out an action plan'* as he had put it to me – perhaps trying to stoke up some kind of rebellion – to what end I did not quite know or understand. There was a lot of misinformation doing the rounds: rumours floated around that everyone below RK's grade (Vice President) would soon be fired because the company did not have any real money to pay our salaries. Or rentals. Or its bills.

The company hadn't had the money for about four years now; the point in time when our esteemed recently jailed CEO in connivance with the CFO began cooking up the financials, overstating profits by thousands of crores. You see big companies do not actually hold money in their wallets or in bank accounts like us normal human beings. They hold it on an intricate extensive piece of paper called the balancesheet, which when you come to think of is incredibly funny. I wish all I needed to do to generate money was to put a random number on a piece of paper. Anyway, once ABCDEF Corp. began cooking up the financials on the balancesheet thingy, the actual numbers started to fall consistently even farther from the blatant untruths. All that the conniving masters could then do was to go on lying, either hoping that their deceit would never get caught or that one day they would luck into some mythical colossal pot of gold which would make their version of the story the actual one magically.

Most people in the office looked as if they would have preferred to walk in to Nazi machine gun fire, to be dead in twenty-two precise mathematically metered minutes. Radhika was wolfing down a chocolate nervously, clearly worried about bigger things than getting fat. The place buzzed with nervous energy; a significant chunk of people had deserted their seats to spend time, glued to the news, in the vicinity of the only TV in the office while an equally significant chunk had decided not to show up to office. The office sizzled with the muted cacophony of unanswered desk phones, unread email pings, with no one even remotely interested in tending to work anymore. RK had sequestered himself in his room and seemed to be doing something on his desktop (as a Vice President one earned the unmatched privilege of owning both a laptop and a desktop); most likely emailing his resume to employment consultants and competitor firms or maybe merely creating one from scratch.

We got an ambiguous email from one of the directors of the board, everyone did, which said things like '…*Whatever happens ,I assure you ABCDEF Corp. will come out stronger!*', '…*not the first conspiracy hatched against this great institution*' and ended with '*Let us come together and join hands to protect the rich legacy of this time honoured company!*' Nobody really gave a plague ridden lab rat's behind about the time honoured company and its rich legacy anymore. It was like General Montgomery saying to those soon-to-be-dead poor sodden US Army soldiers before D Day and Normandy transpired- "If you die, don't worry; our second wave will take care of the Germans."

Amongst the deathward bound undead bastards trolling the office premises, the poorest soddenest of them all were those who had been dim-witted/ ill-fated enough to agree to lock in their bonuses in shares of ABCDEF Corp. stock, which incidentally had crashed from Rs 500 to Rs 5 as soon as the stock markets opened. The "time honoured company with a rich legacy" had this policy wherein you could accept your annual bonus as ESOPs (Employee Stock Options, basically shares in the listed company) with an average lock in of about five years. The objective, as I understand, was employee retention. As of now, all the poor sodden retained undead had locked themselves up in a room with Ogre, discussing their next move.

Around noon, Ogre's group emerged from whatever trench they had earlier descended into. There was a twisted smile on Ogre's face when I met him. I had seen that look before, perhaps; something very very evil was either about to happen or had already happened.

∞

No self respecting human being grows up wanting to be a lowly tossed around and eventually conniving undead minion in a software company. Like millions of boys across India, all Ogre wanted to be, growing up, was an actor, a Bollywood superstar.

Bombay is a cruel miserable place; it takes away your dreams and swallows them in its many seas. City of a million broken hearts, a million scars, a million crushed dreams. Every day, it is estimated, about a thousand people come to Bombay, hoping to be actors. They get off the train, dreams held high on their brows, their sparse baggage on their young shoulders, thinking they are about to walk into Bollywood as soon as they got off. And the damn city awaits like a famished Dementor, ready to rid them off any and every happy memory they could have ever had.

The first thing that hits you as soon as you get off the train is not Bollywood, nor some odd poetic romance certain people (surely mentally sparse) have sought to associate with Bombay, but its filth and stench. Bombay is a haggard old beggar at an intersection who hasn't taken a bath in months; it is not a city with a little bit of slum but a slum with a little bit of city. It breathes its heavy foul smelling happiness sucking breaths unto you and you stagger with the first puff of something you had least expected. This isn't how you envisioned it; this was supposed to be your dream.

Once you have learnt to breathe in that toxic stench, the second thing that hits you is the sheer number of people. Bombay is peopled on every possible square inch of space. There are people everywhere, doing God knows what; people in a perpetual hurry rushing away only God knows where. The damned city yawns, stretches and emits its foul-mouthed stench as you stand dazed and it quakes from the unprecedented and inhuman degree of peopledness.

There is a term for people with high hopes, big dreams and non-existent backup plans who come to Bombay to become actors – *Strugglers*. The day he stepped off the train, Ogre had officially become one. He went to his first audition that very evening, where exhausted from the train ride, he got all his lines wrong. The casting director told him to go back to whichever town he had come from and try for acting roles in the Ram-Leela there.

Audition after audition Ogre went to, he was told that while he could act, he didn't have a hero's face; he should try for roles like the hero's friend (who gets killed in the second scene and becomes the causative for the hero's testosterone fuelled vengeance), or roles having anything to do with villaindom; he apparently looked adequately evil in his six foot five frame. Ogre resigned himself to not becoming a hero but even then hardly any roles came by. Twenty-three auditions and four months of Bombay later, Ogre landed his first role as a henchman for a villain who gets killed by the hero's first bullet. He got seven seconds of screen space and ₹ 500 for his efforts.

Ogre soon learned that the only way to get roles in Bollywood was to be the rich spoilt spawn of a yesteryear Bollywood actor/ producer/ director or to sleep with the casting directors. It was surprising how many casting directors were bisexual and willing to accept sexual favours from either gender. He got indecent proposals from seven out of ten people he approached for movie roles, ranging from the high and mighty to the low and slimy.

Ogre met and befriended a lot of fellow strugglers; they would go to auditions together and post the inevitable rejection or a chance selection, celebrate over sparse roadside food. Ogre told me it was these people that kept him sane and kept him from succumbing and agreeing to sleep with the producers or committing suicide. Some of these people had been 'struggling' in Bollywood for ten years; one of them was a forty-year-old woman who had been struggling for twenty years and had slept with nearly every producer and casting director in the city and could vividly describe each of them in bed.

Ogre told me a lot of Bollywood secrets, one of the few privileges of having had his ear to the ground as a bonafide struggler. For example, the son of a famous liquor baron was gay and a semi-successful young actress had been signed on contract to play his girlfriend, just to keep his image in the Indian media clean and heterosexual. An actor who had once famously bashed up his ex-girlfriend had passed on a rather vicious STD to whichever heroine he had slept around with for about a year. Bollywood apparently was an amazing unbelievable smorgasbord of sexually active unfaithful people, most of whom could not act to save their lives (in Ogre's words), and looked quite hideous without four hours of cosmetic repair.

A struggler in Bollywood lives the worst possible slow-death-by-inhalation-of-carcinogenic-aerosol-over-time kind of existence. Neither can these people go back for fear of being ridiculed by the family or friends they had left behind in their hometowns, nor can they stay and breathe the foul mouthed unforgiving, unrelenting stench of Bombay's Dementor. Over the years, some of them go back, some of them commit suicide, some make a career and a living with itsy bitsy roles, while most hang around without significant Bollywood work – doing day jobs to finance their stay in the bloodsuckingly expensive bloody slum of a city and going to auditions by night; forever living in the incessant hope that they will soon land that role that will change their lives forever. Success is forever lurking just around the corner; just one audition more, just one indecent proposal more, *soon I'll be noticed in my ten second role, soon I'll have the big flat and big car in one of those bloody sea-facing high rises, soon I'll be the one passing on STDs to nubile young actresses.*

Ogre struggled for one whole year. In that one year, he was thrice the villain's henchman, five times a dancer in the back row in an item number, once a model on *Emotional Attyachar* who failed to attract the girlfriend away from her boyfriend (thereby making it the first case in the history of the show where the suspected cheater actually stayed faithful), and finally a villain in what was clearly his best rôle in a B grade movie. During his thirty minutes of on-screen villainry, Ogre killed five people and raped two women singlehandedly; clearly an achievement worthy of a mention in something like a B school interview form.

My mission and vision in life is to kill men and rape women. Period.

Fuck you.

He had had that evil twisted look on his face all through the movie.

The turning point came when Ogre was to play a shopkeeper in a big budget movie. He had one dialogue in the movie and was to be reimbursed a princely sum of rupees two thousand for it; equivalent presently to six hundred and sixty six point six seven of my trips to the urinal at ABCDEF Corp.

"*Ek hazaar pachaas hua, madam.*"

'Madam' – a pretty young thing who was rumoured to be the hero's latest extramarital plaything – turned up four hours late for the shoot. Ogre by then had rehearsed about two hundred and fifty odd ways of saying that one sentence, each incremental version intended as a carefully calibrated projectile aimed at landing that one big superstar birthing role.

When madam finally turned up, she looked exhausted, hung over and fucked up in general. The assistant directors were dispatched to find cucumbers for madam's dark circles and beauticians were sought to unflaw her flawed beauty.

After one-and-a-half hours of cosmetic restoration, madam finally appeared for the first take. In the scene, madam was supposed to be talking on the phone as she walked up to Ogre – the supermarket checkout counter guy – with her bag of groceries. Ogre would then work a bar code reader on her groceries' tags while she continued to talk with love interest telephonically, growing more and more emotional by the minute as she was, per the script, being broken up with. Ogre would then project that carefully metered missile that was to (finally) launch his career in Bollywood: "*Ek hazaar pachaas hua madam*", hand over the grocery bag to her, following which madam, clearly shattered by her recent telephonic break up would dramatically drop the damn bag to the floor. Shattered heart. Shattered milk bottles. Classic cringe-worthy Bollywood metaphor.

But try as she might, madam couldn't get the scene right. She kept forgetting her dialogues or screwing up their delivery. Finally after fifty odd takes and fifteen odd shattered milk bottles, with the scene not yet wrapped up, madam yelled, "Enough… That's it! Pack up!"

The director almost had a heart attack. Producing an average Bollywood movie costs about ten to fifteen crore rupees. I knew this because Ogre knew this. If say the movie is made on a fifteen crore budget within a three month schedule, every day of the shoot costs 16.67 lakhs. That's sixteen fucking lakhs for one day. That's too much piss for any urinal to handle.

Rattled, the assistant directors and the director rushed up to madam and tried to persuade her to continue shooting but she remained unmoved.

But this was not what turned Ogre. He had seen shooting delays and superstar tantrums before. Hell, one of the item number starlets he had worked with earlier had demanded that only bottled mineral water be used for the rain dance sequence and the producers had eventually complied, buying out a month's stock from the local stockist of Bisleri, making some newbie MBA salesguy somewhere very happy. What turned him was when madam, in the middle of her conversation with the director and his lackeys, turned to him and said, "Get me some juice from my van, will you?"

There was a blinding hot lightning strike in Ogre's head. Same as, I imagine, when he found out that those jokers had taken his monies saved in ABCDEF Corp. stock and left it more worthless than a steaming pile of cow dung.

How dare the fucking piece of trash order him around for juice?

Silently, Ogre walked over to the nearest juice counter (they were shooting in an actual supermarket in Bandra), picked out an apple juice and did his thing.

I like to think he had that evil twisted look on his face.

Madam accepted the glass of juice from him without a word or glance. As he walked away from her and out of the supermarket, determined never to return again Ogre heard madam remark "…too warm."

At this point, I like to think Ogre had a smile on his face, one befitting a villain whose vision and mission statement in life was to kill men and rape women.

Ogre landed the first job he interviewed for, got through the group discussion and then the damn interview. The engineering degree had always been the fallback. Ogre had fallen back.

And when he told me the story, he looked at the aghast expression on my face triumphantly, a look of triumph befitting a B- grade Hindi movie villain and said, "Madam is safe, don't worry, no lasting damage done. Thought you are a chemical engineer...

Don't you know urine is completely sterile?"

I only know this because Ogre told me this.

The Vengeance of Ogre

Ogre had started a cult.
There is really no better way to put that.

The cult met every weekday at our flat and then on weekends, seven to nine, after work and could be called – for lack of a more fitting description – "Disgruntled employees of ABCDEF Corp."

At work, we were saving cost. The pantry was out of biscuits, the stationery room out of stationery, and the toilets out of toilet paper and liquid soap. Investors in the company's GDR in the US and Europe had sued for billions and the company was hoarding and/or selling toilet paper and liquid soap to cover litigation costs.

At home, the cult was making plans. There was a Legal Wing. An Internal Petition Wing. A Spy Wing. A Finance Wing. And a Mischief and Misinformation Wing.

There was even a spokesperson. In classic spokesperson style, he said "No Comments" when I asked him how I could join the Mischief and Misinformation Wing.

The next day, the entire office was covered in toilet paper. Not just *all* the interior floors but the outside of the building too had toilet paper covering the front in streaks of white, unfurled off the roof. On the glass façade at the front, someone had spray painted "NO MORE SHIT!" in an impossible to miss huge red font. There was a traffic jam outside the office as people stopped to get a better look and/ or take pictures.

Ogre looked the happiest and evil-est I had ever seen him in my life. The cult had a celebratory dinner that evening.

A couple of days later, we had something a tad less spectacular, but far funnier. The first email that popped up when we arrived to work was from the acting CEO (appointed after the ex-CEO's arrest) and said "MODERFUCJARS! YOU ARE ALL GOING TO DIE!" Not just this, a couple of directors from the board seemed to have replied on the email to a similar effect. "Dieeeee Bitchhhhhhhes" one of them had opined. Another board member declared "GAY AND PROUD!" One more expressed the desire to '*fornicate with a dog or anything with four legs and a tail that can wag*'.

To this day, honest to God, I have no clue how they did this one. My suspicion was that they had somehow gotten to the secretaries or the assistants of these senior guys but despite my asking him a hundred times, Ogre never confirmed or refuted my theory. A high level team, that included RK, was set up to investigate the incidents but they found out nothing. Zilch. Not one spoke up. RK promptly handed down his part of the investigation to me, telling me *he had other more important things to do.* Like maybe search for a job. Or be evil in general.

I had never really been a part of the cult (Ogre had told me people needed to have lost a significant chunk of their savings in ABCDEF Corp. stock to join; that was the sole joining criterion) but with me getting pseudo appointed on the investigation committee for both the events, I got pushed even further apart. Ogre forbade me completely from participating in even a single meeting or being privy to even the slightest hint of their next plans. I was to be either outside the house or sequestered in my room whenever they met. Whenever I could, I took to spying on them through the keyhole. But they talked in murmurs and I could never really make much out.

After the two event blitzkrieg, the mischief scene however went cold even though the cult met with clockwork regularity every day. RK had cc'ed me on the investigation thread, whose only achievement had been to find proof(s) that all possible proofs had been destroyed. There were no fingerprints, no eyewitnesses, the CCTV cameras had all been switched off before the toilet paper incident, the secretaries were vehemently denying their involvement in the email scandal (but were placed on suspension anyway).

I was only half listening as Sudeep explained to me how Pay-Day was still on track. I could not help but admire how well he was handling the project; he had actually made a presentation on it without my even asking for it. I felt hungover and tired and stared at him blankly feeling almost certain that I had spotted him through the keyhole the previous evening.

He had just begun explaining to me how they had debugged the software when I interrupted him with "Were you there at my house last night?"

He looked as if thrown off track. After a three second pause, he said "No" but his eyes looked shifty as if unsure whether to speak the truth or mirror his lie. We labored through the rest of his presentation, Sudeep going through it jerkily cognizant now of the elephant I had ushered into the room.

I asked him a couple of questions on Pay-Day as he finished and satisfied with his answers let him go. Just as he was walking out of my cubicle, I said suddenly, "When's the next prank?"

He turned suddenly as if caught off guard and stopped himself from saying something that I thought he was going to say. He then smiled and said something which made no sense, "But you already know that, don't you?"

I spent the next half hour trying to drown my confusion in the politics section of *The Hindu*. Bored completely and mentally spent, I decided to walk over to RK and warn him my two week B-school interview leave was starting the next day, so he better let me know if there was some last minute work left. RK was on a conference call when I walked in and asked me to sit and wait. I sat in the comfortable sofa and nearly fell asleep. Fifteen minutes later, with no end to the con-call in site, I scribbled my message on a post it and passed it on to him. The half-addled chimpanzee almost rebooted with the multitasking requirement reading a post-it note while speaking on a call presented. But the message somehow registered and RK gestured for me to leave. No 'Thank You'. No 'Best of luck'. As I walked out the door, I heard him say "…we have found some incriminating evidence."

I decided to warn Ogre whenever I saw him. As I walked out of the building into the afternoon sun only for the second time in my career, I prayed to God that I was seeing the damn office for the last time.

I looked back and saw some cleaners hard at work on the façade. They had succeeded in removing one complete word and now the façade said simply, succinctly and maybe even prophetically (now that I come to think of it) "MORE SHIT!"

Blackhead

I have no idea how and why the employees at "Nice Hair Saloan, Vile Parle West" (*Yes 'Saloan' and not 'Salon'*) kept changing. I couldn't recall the face of one single barber even though I visited the place once every month for shaving and hair related emergencies. This time, however, I had gone for two-and-a-half odd months without a haircut or a shave (as a result of having given up completely on my non-existent career at ABCDEF Corp.) and was being told that I had begun to look like a Brazilian footballer from the '80s', what with all the hair on my face and the hair behind my neck tied into a small pointy ponytail with a cheap rubber band that comes with the morning newspaper.

The barber assigned to me recognized me even though I had no idea who he was or what planet he had descended from. He asked me how work was going to which I think I mumbled something monosyllabic before throwing the question back at him, rather rhetorically. Barber 1 however wasn't as discreet as me and took ten minutes to take me through the woes of a hair salonist – from rising input costs to lack of trained motivated haircutters (*for whom hair cutting was a calling in life*, he used these exact words in Hindi, I kid you not) to the declining quality of human hair which reduced the reimbursement the Nice Hair Saloan got from selling off human hair to wigmakers. Apparently, barbershops make more than 50% of their profits from selling human hair. They barely break even on the operational side of the business. Without my even asking, Barber 1 gave me a quarterly business review of his haircutting op. The Nice Hair Saloan was profitable enough for me to consider a career in haircutting. Fleetingly.

By the time I had had my hair done and turned down the barber's many requests to get a shoulder massage or a facial pack (he pointed out the fact that my face had several *blackheads* to try and convince me, whatever that meant), I had a good enough overview of the business of haircutting to write a business plan on it.

My mission and vision in life is to be a haircutter and to tell people they have blackheads.

I said *No thanks* and that *I had one black head and I liked it that way*. Barber 1 looked bemused and let me go.

Next stop was the shoe store. Bombay's humidity ensures that whatever garment, shoe, pen, notebook, electrical gadget or vehicle you own, dies an untimely death, much before it would in any other city. My shoes bought in my hometown had lasted a good three years (with help from the local cobbler). My last shoes lasted no more than six months. It did not help that I had to wade through flood waters for one entire month of monsoon in them.

The shoestore salesman made a righteous fuss about getting me those magical leather boots that could land me a place in one of India's finest B-schools. He took one long look at my foot (frowned at the rubber flip fops I was wearing) and shouted out at his errand boy to get him model X512, AB212, C124 in black and so on.

The models having been furnished, he hooked me up with a couple of pointy toed leather shoes which looked as if they had belonged to a big footed clown. He convinced me that they were *"in"* these days. I put my feet *in* them and felt the sudden urge to get up, point at my cherry-red-balled nose, gesture to the crowd and begin laughing hysterically. I asked Shoeman to quit screwing around and get me some normal shoes meant for human beings.

Normal shoes arrived and fit beautifully. Just as I was about to close off the sale, he told me the shoes were manufactured by some Berluti person and that they were for Rs 18000.

The total cost of all the shoes I had ever worn in my life did not add up to Rs 18000.

I asked him who Berluti was. He had no clue. I felt certain the damn guy was an MBA.

I walked into the Bata showroom next door and got myself unfunny black leather boots for one tenth the price.

I walked home wearing the shoes. Just as I had gotten home, the washerman arrived with my shirt and trouser set – spic, span and ironed.

I put on the shirt over my T shirt and pajamas, and still wearing my leather boots, walked up to the mirror. There was a reddish patch on my neck which I had no memory of. Despite the patch, I looked about five years younger; as if I had just returned to civilization after having been shipwrecked and cast away for a good one year.

I felt ready for the first interview.

Part Three Begins

The End Begins

The Woman

The doorbell woke me up. Unlike other days, it did not set off a cacophony of jungle bird sounds in my head; I had been sober for at least 24 hours.

I got up from the bed, still exhausted from the one last late night study session I had subjected myself to. Except a few major events in the last couple of weeks (which included ABCDEF Corp.'s sudden bust), my current affairs were more or less current. The major stickler had been chemistry yet again, which I had somehow contrived to forget quite significantly. Those bloody chemicals in Jain & Jain sucked up three hours of my sleep time and I finally had gone to sleep at 3 a.m. post taking a quick shower and laying out my interview paraphernalia – shirt, tie, shoes, socks and a professional looking CV folder which I had shamelessly stolen from RK's cabin.

The jungle bird in our doorbell squawked again, the squawk this time sounding more desperate than the last. I yawned, stretched and began to make my way groggily to the door. Ogre was nowhere to be seen. The clock in the living room told me it was noon, which meant there were more or less three hours to go to my IIT Bombay MBA interview, just the perfect amount of time considering Powai was not more than a half hour auto ride from our place. I paused before the door for a second to scratch my butt and say a silent prayer to God that it was a Domino's delivery boy at the door.

I opened the door and froze. I like to think that if I were to have seen my face in the mirror at this point, I would have a seen a guy from one of those '*Shock Laga*' commercials – mouth half open in an almost scream, eyes open and frozen wide, hair standing on edge, breath stuck in throat. For at the door stood a sobbing Ira Sharma.

The woman barged in leaving me standing at the door in her wake. I stood motionless and without thought for one entire minute before scanning the hall outside finding no sign of Ogre – who I assumed was the cause of her distress – before walking back in. She sat on our sofa, sobbing away softly, almost politely.

I stood for a few seconds "Ogre's not here," I said quietly.

She did not react.

I then realized most probably she did not call him that.

"Ryan's not here," I repeated softly. But she continued sobbing as if she had not heard.

Over time, I had honed my ability of dealing with

weeping women. It was suicide to comfort them, for that would only increase the intensity of their displayed sorrow. It was also suicide to try and reason with them for, well, the obvious and reasonable thing to do was to not cry at all. When accosted by a teary eyed female, one is thus well advised to simply sit and wait it out.

So while the woman sat on our sofa ejecting tears, I took out a beer and began to consume it quietly. I went through two bottles and she did not even look up. She just sat in an awkward pose, head facing down, weeping away with decorum. It was 12:30 now and I wanted to leave as quickly as possible. Before moving off to get dressed, however, I decided to offer her a glass of water, perhaps the most socially acceptable method of pacifying someone.

She accepted the water and drank it eagerly, almost hungrily.

"I have to go," I said once she was finished. "Why don't you make yourself comfortable here?"

Her eyes met mine for the first time since she had made her dramatic entry and I saw she was in real pain. She opened her mouth as if to say something but then stopped herself, "OK... go," she said.

I switched the TV on for her and handed her the remote. There was some movie on about a really grotesque baby with a man's face; it was probably supposed to be funny.

"There's beer and some food in the fridge," I said. She nodded without looking at me.

I left the woman alone to take a quick shower and get dressed. The professional looking CV folder went into a professional looking bag; the ties, socks and other interview paraphernalia went on me. I stood before the bathroom mirror for a good five minutes telling myself today was my day and that the weeping woman was not an omen from God. For good measure, however, I bowed before my copy of Jain & Jain to appease the Gods of Chemistry at the very least. I also lit up an incense stick superstitiously and stuck it into the book, silently hoping that the damn thing would burn up by the time I returned.

When I stepped out of my enclosure, I saw that the woman had opened up one of those beer bottles and was sipping it slowly, whilst watching the life story of the grotesque man-baby with mild interest. She saw me and said, "This tastes funny" with a faint smile. Were we friends now?

I brushed my confusion aside and gave her a blanket and a pillow. Like the spoilt XYZ-ian for life she was, she let me open the blanket for her and wrap her folded legs in it whilst sipping beer. She took the pillow from me and put it by her side so that she came to rest on it.

"Okay, I'll be leaving now," I said pulling away and she said nothing. "If you want to leave, leave everything as it is. And the door locks itself once closed."

I walked away and just as I was at the door, she said softly and with the slightest tinge of alcohol induced cheer in her voice, "Best of luck."

I flinched instinctively. As omens go, I felt sure this was not a good one.

൞

It took me some time to find an auto. The trick in Bombay while househunting is to find a house that is adequately far away from any and every location you can think of going to, so that your fare gives a decent profit margin to the autowallah. For example, say your office is in Bandra, it would then be public-transport-suicide if you took an apartment in the vicinity of Bandra on rent, for no self respecting autowallah would ever agree to ferry you for a fifteen buck fare.

Even though Powai was a good fifty bucks away from our house, it took me ten minutes to find an auto. It was probably a strike; they kept having them there. The autowallah thankfully quietly smoked a bidi and did not bother me with his life story like the hair salon-ist. I rested my head on the yellow tarp that made the top half of the contraption and closed my eyes. But try as I might, my head did not clear. My mind was a montage of thoughts – of hurriedly mugged up chemistry, of riots and revolutions in nations I hadn't heard of a year ago, of the staleness and sameness of Bombay's pathetic existence, of that beautiful bewitching beauty stuck in my head – my memory from a life before. In fact, the more I tried to untangle the knots in my head, the more they got tangled; they reproduced and multiplied and cross-fertilized. Every thought was now a montage in itself and I was more anxious and nervous now than when the journey had started.

The auto weaved in and out of traffic jerkily, the driver smoking his bidi all the time, unmoved and unstirred, like a nicotine guzzling perpetual motion machine. My thoughts bounced like marbles in a grinder jar colliding with each other noisily and injuriously – churning and shattering and bouncing and sanding pieces off each other. By the time we were done, my head was a jar of sand and I felt completely exhausted.

When I got off at IIT Bombay, I felt nervous, mentally exhausted and shattered from the sand in my head. I let the auto-man off with his fifty bucks and he disappeared into the innards of the slum city.

Powai was one of the few places in Bombay that, depending on the time of the year, did not carry its stench or carried it rather mutedly (everything stinks in the monsoons). The fact that it was dotted with European style buildings carved out of the hills by the Hiranandanis helped. Powai was very unBombay – a picturesque lake, hills dotted with greenery, cobbled streets and at first glance slum free beautiful historical looking buildings.

The IIT Bombay campus had the setting of a resort. It flanked the lake and had more trees than a damn rainforest; so many in fact that they had almost entirely blocked out the sun. I realized my mistake in a couple of minutes; I should have gotten the auto to drive in and drop me at the

Convention Centre because it was a good kilometre-and-a-half inside the campus.

By the time I reached the Convention Centre, I had begun to sweat through my shirt from Bombay's relentless humidity. At the Centre were gathered some hundred odd applicants in an army of black suits. I saw that I was amongst the handful who had chosen to give the suit a miss and hang all his fate on just a tie. People sipped some kind of fruit drink that was being passed around and mingled and chatted with each other freely. I made my way to a glass of juice and got promptly accosted by someone in an "IIT Rocks" T Shirt and shorts, apparently a senior.

IIT-man introduced himself and shook my hand congenially. Across the hall I saw several other seniors mingling around with the suit-folk. I sipped my juice quietly and let IIT-man say good things about his campus. Finally he said he had to go and introduced me to a circle of five kids, interviewees all of them, who seemed to be exchanging information on CAT scores, number of calls and whatnot.

If you are a general category engineering campus ejected male, your chances of getting selected in an interview diminish dramatically, simply because there are so many others like you. Take an XYZ-ian for life (and hence non engineering campus ejected), good looking female instead and you needn't even worry about the number of interview calls you get, for you will convert every one of them. There was this thing going that had been going around in

B-schools for some time – 'Diversity'. Apparently, having an engineering degree and being the spawn of human beings not belonging to any caste or tribe christened *scheduled* or *backward* by the Indian government, and possessing a penis, screwed up B-school diversity. If you had a penis and worse still, a general category engineering campus penis, you could just sit and hope and pray that not wearing a suit to an interview where 95% of people had been foolish enough to wear one in Bombay's bloodsucking humidity made you stand out.

We were eventually led like cattle to a spacious room wherein we were supposed to submit some documents and get a couple of forms filled. All this time, seniors kept mingling with us trying to talk us in to the IIT experience – of how IIT Bombay was the only ragging free B-school in the country. I pictured myself in an IIT Rocks T-shirt and shorts and begun calming my frayed nerves.

By the time a Bengali looking guy who spoke with a South Indian accent showed up and called out my name for the Group Discussion, I was only slightly calmer than I had been at the IIT gates. However, I was now more pumped instead of nervous; adrenaline gushed through my veins and I looked at the queue of twelve that had formed around me with a condescending aggression which one only tends to regret in retrospect.

We marched in single file towards our destination. People tightened their ties and straightened their collars, tucked in their tummies and buttoned their suits, pasted errant hairs to their scalps and involuntarily flicked dandruff out of their hair. A couple even mock gargled their throats the way singers tend to do before concerts.

We were stopped at the entrance of a room surely too small to house twelve people and the South Indian-Bengali human mash-up read out and ticked off our names on his list. We then entered – lambs to the slaughter – ties straightened, hair pasted, throats cleared and/ or gargled, bellies tucked in. There was not one woman in our group which I hoped was a sign of deliverance from God. This however also meant that every one of the bastards in the room was potentially a desperate engineering campus bred general category penis like me, which is never a good thing.

When we entered, there were two other people seated in the room already, who looked old and distinguished enough to be professors or some other species belonging to the moderator/ interviewer genus. The South Indian Bengali ensured that we sat down in a particular order and that big cloth napkins with numbers on them got pinned to the front of our clothes. I was number seven, which if my memory served right, was the number of the devil per this Jim Carrey movie I had seen last week.

The older of the two old men cleared his throat and asked us to take two minutes and read the case in front of us and then start discussing it. We would have 12 minutes to discuss it, one minute for every group member.

So we read the case in front of us. People around me took out pencils and pens and began underlining, circling words, taking notes even. I saw that the case was four pages long printed in a cruelly small font and virtually impossible to read in three minutes. In a split second foreign beer induced flash of (perhaps) genius, I realized that this clearly was the trick. They would throw something between us twelve hounds, bloodthirsty and raring to go and all of us would immediately pounce on it, only to realize much later that it was poison by which time the damage would already have been done.

The questions at the end confirmed my theory. They were at the bottom of page three, nestled inconspicuously beneath three and three quarters pages of crap. They had nothing to do with the two and a half pages I had read and instead only obliquely referred to whatever I had read. I looked up at the wise old men and caught them smiling at the little joke they had played on us. My eyes and that of the older wiser one met and in that instant he roared "Time's up! START!"

The idiot numbered three started instantly. He began summarizing the crap he had managed to read in two minutes which I realized was about one page less than me. He had just about spoken two and a half sentences when someone begged to differ with him. This was idiot number two seated on three's left. Idiot number two had been smart enough to read the questions at least while being unable to finish reading the case. He managed to get the first question at the end read out aloud before all hell broke loose. In the normal saner environment practice group discussions I had attended in the human world, there would be speech gaps between people shouting, screaming, squabbling that you could exploit; or my favourite tactic – generally after the first speaker would have spoken, two people (or sometimes three) would speak up together cancelling each other out – at which point I had trained myself to enter. On Planet Stupid however pandemonium reigned, four people began speaking at the same time cutting off Idiot Three and did not shut up for one split second. This went on for what seemed like eternity; my head felt like it was stuck in a bad hangover.

Finally, I banged the table and got up. The four idiots and a fifth one who had added himself to the cacophony in the last ten seconds, all simultaneously shut up. "SHUT UP!" I shouted.

There was a stunned silence. The old men looked at me bemused.

"HAS ANY ONE OF YOU EVEN READ THE WHOLE THING!" I continued shouting.

Idiot Two began stammering a reply. "NO YOU HAVEN'T," I shouted back.

I took a breath and calmed down. "I suggest we take a two minute break, finish the case and then and only then begin discussing it." The stunned silence persevered.

Nobody moved an inch, unsure of what to do next. I sat down and gestured dramatically towards the case and said quietly, "Read! Please."

But no one read. Idiot number twelve instantly jumpstarted the discussion again and the herd was back in – kicking and flailing – hoping something hit, something registered on the scoreboards of the old wise men. My adrenaline receded, my head began throbbing and my brain gave up. I put my head in my hands and sat quietly waiting for the sham to get over.

It seemed only a couple of minutes had passed when one of the old men shouted "Time's up!"

The idiots however did not shut up. Two of them – Five and Twelve – continued to bicker over summarizing the case.

"Time's up!" the older wiser man exclaimed again. "Please leave."

I got up and walked out of the room before anyone else could, clutching the damn stapled case sheets in my hand. The throbbing in my head felt worse. I walked out of the structure into fading sunlight and closed my eyes inhaling deeply lungfuls of Bombay's pollution laden farce of fresh air.

I closed my eyes and pushed my head back, breathing slow deep breaths. I felt a smidgen of peace wash over me, the tiniest bit.

And in that moment of peace, I felt strong hands reach out from behind me. They thrust a weird smelling cloth in my face and for some reason I did not struggle. An arm reached out from behind too, semi throttling my neck. I inhaled deeply as before and submitted myself to whoever had taken a violent fancy to me, quickly descending into an abyss made of pitch black unconsciousness.

The Dark Black

Ihad never seen blackness so black. I drank it in, letting it envelope me completely, cut me off from my world of miseries and worries and regrets and memories. I threw it a deep embrace and the darkness clutched me back. It held me to its bosom possessively and I stayed in; at least the dark was predictable.

My senses awoke in parts. First came smell. My nose told me I was surrounded by the odor of sweat. That was not really a surprise; 24 hour deodorants weren't really made for Bombay's humidity.

Next came sound. I heard a lot of noise, none of it making much sense at first. I heard people speak and I recognized the fact that the language was familiar but still couldn't piece together what the words meant.

And then came touch and with it a sense of awkward to and fro motion. My awakening senses told me I was in a reeking incoherently noisy spacecraft floating jerkily and bouncing away weightlessly off what felt like balloons.

I was an asteroid bouncing off two trampoline planets.

I was a crazy ball a sweaty kid was bouncing off his bedroom walls.

I felt a slap.

The crazy ball stopped bouncing momentarily.

"*Mar to nai gaya?*"

Another slap followed and I orbited around to the second trampoline planet with the impact.

Big fat callus ridden hands grabbed my neck and the planet who owned the hands announced "*Pulse hai… Zinda hai saala.*"

As the hands began to move away, a singular callus hit my Adam's apple hard and finally activated my sight. Finally all my senses converged into one confusing smorgasbord of confusing sensory mish-mash.

I found myself – erstwhile semi-comatose and still attempting to gain hold of the involuntary pendulum like motions of my body – bouncing between the magnificently round protruding bellies of two men. The men wore what appeared to be police uniforms and one of them held an almost unbelievably long ancient looking rifle I felt sure did not actually work. They reeked of sweat and cheap gutka.

I was a crazy ball asteroid in a Milky Way of ancient rifles and the stench of sweat.

I was a general category engineering campus eject and B-school prospect in a tie in a police van.

৪০

My hands were not handcuffed. Surely this was a good sign.

Instead of handcuffing me, the two morbidly obese policemen held me by each hand as if I was some kind of lost child.

Surely there had been some mistake.

Surely I had not been arrested for my group discussion tirade... or had I?

I trudged along groggily with the policemen clutching on to their hands. I was led into a dilapidated structure that called itself Khar Police Station. I was deposited in a wooden chair and the fat men promptly turned and left. There was a sleepy man at an adjoining ancient wooden table staring blankly into space, his head resting on his right hand. I felt like a lost child.

Ogre knew a lot of useless stuff. He told me once- *put pressure on the carotid artery (the one in your neck) for six seconds and any man will go to sleep for a long long time.* What he hadn't told me was how much the neck would hurt post regaining consciousness. I could still feel a ghost hand clutching on to my throat. The soporific hawaldar looked at me with sleepy interest as I gagged and stretched open my jaws to fight the pervasive choking sensation.

A familiar looking middle aged man with a slight paunch came and sat in front of me.

"Hello. Remember me?" he said in English tinged with a Marathi accent.

I let my gagging throat be and focused my faculties on the policeman in front of me. The newest entrant to the story was actually the same SI who had walked into RK's room on the fateful night his sedan had exploded. His nametag described him as "SHO Marak Ingle".

"Understand Marathi?" he asked.

I shook my head and croaked "No" with difficulty.

Clearly this was the wrong answer. SI/ SHO Ingle scowled and continued in English.

"You have been doing bad things, haven't you?" he said stretching out 'baaaaaad' like chewing gum.

I just stared at him with wonder, my throat still incapable of making intelligent sounds.

"We have been following you… you and your friends for some time now, my friend," he continued. "Doing some bad baaaaaad stuff, aren't we?"

So this was about Ogre's cult. I wished I had never gotten drunk at that induction party, never even met him. I wished to close my eyes and un-know all that I knew of Ogre and his world.

"I'll tell you everything," I opened my mouth and attempted to say.

Only what came out from my semi-throttled throat was the sound of a monsoon frog croaking away merrily.

The frog sound did not go down well with Ingle. He thumped the table with such genuine passion that the soporific hawaldar almost woke up.

"The day I met you I knew you were a criminal… twenty years of police work," he said proudly thumping the table and then his chest, "*twenty years* of instinct is never wrong."

The police corporate ladder was clearly screwed up. Twenty years and Ingle had only risen to a Sub Inspector; the rank itself seemed to imply sub-standard. If I had had my throat, aside from telling him everything about Ogre's activities, I would have advised him to do an MBA.

Ingle now held the *twenty years* like an imaginary heavy tray made of metal in front of him and repeated waving his imaginary tray-holding hands up and down "Twenty years!"

He then reached out across his table and held me by the collar and snarled angrily at me, "Tell me how you blew up that car!"

This was a startling new development; Ingle had clearly made me a suspect in the RK's sedan explosion investigation. But even this level of drama did not arouse interest from the sleepy hawaldar; he just stared at the borderline funny scene of Ingle – presumably his boss – semi prostrated across the length of his desk to reach my collar.

I opened my mouth to express surprise but only a croak came out.

I saw a Reynolds pen sticking out at an acute angle from under Ingle's paunch. Erect at a weird angle like an emaciated plastic penis.

Ingle grew angrier when he got no verbal response from me and began jerking me by the collar. I counterbalanced the weight of his hands by rocking back and forth with his jerks, primarily to avoid any further pressure on my already impacted neck. This, as it turned out however, was not really the brightest idea.

Ingle grew so frustrated by his *twenty year old* tactic not working that he gave me one almighty collar tug backwards, the force of which I let my body consume. This meant that as he tugged me back, my entire body moved back along with the chair at great speed. And in that one moment of panic when I realized that I was about to fall backwards, I grabbed the first thing I could think of with my flailing arms to break my impending fall, which in this case were Ingle's forearms. The sheer force of the tug-induced motion was such that not only did I fall backwards in my wooden chair pendulum, I dragged Ingle along with me across the table and onto the ground.

The chair promptly broke from the impact and Ingle and I lay on the floor amidst the debris like confused cartoon characters from a Tom & Jerry cartoon.

"What's happening?" exclaimed a familiar voice.

I looked through the cartoon like web of arms and legs, some human, some wooden; I was entangled in and failed to locate the owner of the voice even though I had recognized it. That singular evil female voice.

I did see the hawaldar though fully awake and standing

upright looking at the scene before him with mild interest. "Oh Ingle sahib," he moaned softly.

Ingle sahib lay with half his paunch on top of me unconscious, his left arm covering my head. I felt his phlegm obstructed breath on my chest. With some effort, I pushed him off me and sat upright. He came to rest on the ground, facing floorwards, his breath raising circles of dust from the Khar police station floor in mini tornadoes.

Ira Sharma looked at me with a look a little too complicated to describe. For one moment, the sunlight hit her face at a particular angle and she looked almost as mesmerizing as the mysterious beauty of my past life.

Almost.

"Get up," she said quietly. A cloud came over the sun and the moment passed.

I got up groggily. Ingle still lay on the floor in a deep slumber, breathing deeply.

My mission and vision in life is to leave policemen in a coma.

I stared at the hawaldar who seemed unsure of what to do next.

"We're leaving," she said to me.

The hawaldar stayed mesmerized by his comatose boss and did not react.

I started to walk towards the exit when he said something in Marathi that sounded like he wanted me to stop.

Ira Sharma said something back to him in Marathi which

I did not understand. But I understood the tone – acidic, vile and bitter.

Clearly this was too much excitement for the hawaldar's little brain and it almost shut down.

He responded in Marathi, more politely this time. I almost understood what he had said. "No he has not been arrested."

Ira gave him a mock bow – a mark of sarcastic gratitude – and gestured for me to follow.

So I followed. I could not speak; there was a throbbing bruise on the back of my head, the now dried sweat of three policemen was pasted on my body and some wood particles and termites resided on my back.

I was dazed and confused but felt strangely thankful to the woman. We just walked out of the police station, me following in her wake, as if nothing had happened.

Behind me, I heard Ingle snore loudly.

౮

I was in the frame of mind to believe in dragons and gods and feng shui and fairytales. There were too many random events happening around for my brain to process.

I craved alcohol.

Ira Sharma drove as if she was in a hurry. Her evil red little car weaved in and out of traffic lanes, almost always a centimetre away from hitting a car bumper or a motorcycle or polishing off a pedestrian.

"Did you really blow up your boss' car?" she asked.

I attempted to reply which set off an incessant rasping cough.

She looked at my eyes – not really a great idea when driving the way she was – and saw the confusion in them and got her answer. Perhaps.

"They came to my house earlier too, you know, asking about you," she said. "I said I didn't know you."

I croaked out a semi-audible "Who?"

"Them… the police," she said simply.

She didn't know me. Period.

My mission and vision in life is to crave alcohol and believe in dragons.

"And then they came back when you had just left today. I sort of wanted to screw you over, so I told them where you were," she said, matter-of-factly.

The evil red car weaved in and out like in the joystick controlled video game from my childhood. I never ever crossed Level One. I just realized that that was my deepest regret.

"…And then I began to feel guilty. So I figured out which police station they were from," she continued.

Ira Sharma had most definitely mastered the joystick video game with the little red car. For her five rupees pocket money, she would have played ten levels in one go as opposed to my one.

Ira Sharma most definitely had no deep seated videogame related regrets.

The car weaved in and out still as it did towards the end of Level One, the point where I always lost.

"There's bribe money in the glove compartment... but as it turns out, didn't need it," she went on.

I opened the glove compartment and saw there was a moderately thick bundle of cash there.

And then she said bitterly, "You know you are an asshole, don't you?"

At this point, I believed in feng shui and dragons and fairytales and the alignment of planets impacting our everyday lives and I was henceforth, for the foreseeable future, immune to surprises. I felt inclined to agree. I even nodded, perhaps.

The little red car from the videogame consumed Ira's anger, bopping from one lane to the other, forever a centimetre away from kissing another vehicle and causing Level One to end.

And then suddenly, she stopped the car right in the middle of the road. I heard brakes being applied suddenly and vehicles screeching to a halt.

"You are an asshole and you deserve to die!" she suddenly screamed at me angrily.

People horned from behind us. Ira thrust her arm out and gave the guy in the car behind us the finger.

She pulled the same hand back in put it on my left cheek. I saw there was a teardrop in her right eye.

She then leaned in as a mechanic does to check a damaged tyre rim.

The first moment I realized something was wrong was when her face got too close to mine for comfort. And then she was no longer interested in checking out the damaged rim. The second moment of shock hit me when her eyes closed.

Much like most of the events in the past couple of hours, I had not foreseen this either.

Her lips reached mine and she bit them instantly, like fangs dipping into human skin. Her nails dug into my cheek drawing out blood. I felt her breathe heavily as she kissed me fiercely, with immense venom.

She pulled away, her teeth and fingernails snatching away layers of my skin, and blood with them.

"Goodbye… asshole," she said bitterly.

I realized this was my cue to leave.

I opened her evil red door and got out, looking like a mauled animal that belonged at the bottom of every foreseeable food chain.

And in my head played the metallic female voice that lived in the video game machine.

End of Level One.

Insert coin to continue.

The Indigenous Ice Hypothesis

The security guard at our building told me that the constable on the lookout for me had gotten tired of waiting and had asked him to call the station in case I turned up.

He told me simply that he had a family of five to support and that his price was five hundred bucks.

Per day.

He also asked me if a dog had attacked my face.

There was no sign of Ogre in the apartment. His room was completely empty; everything was gone. It was almost as if he did not exist.

I walked into my room to check and found that the damn chemistry bible had not burnt up as I had hoped it would. It just lay there like an indestructible ode to chemical divinity, not the least bit flustered by arson oriented incense sticks and the confusion in its owner's life.

There was still no sign of Ogre.

There was no Ogre in the bathroom either but piled up

in the side were snow white packets of God-only-knew-what. They were stacked in 10 neat stacks by the wall of the shower tub.

I picked up one of them and saw that it called itself "Ice pack".

I suddenly felt as if the stack had always been there… like a silent forgotten conversation that you can remember remnants of.

I walked up to the wash basin and immersed my head under flowing tap water. I wanted to drown, to get washed down swirling round and round down the wash basin drain. When I emerged eventually from under the water, five minutes later, I was oddly calmer from the thought of my impending inevitable destruction. The fatality rate of every human being I had heard of had always been a hundred per cent. Everyone dies.

I pictured myself dying in a shower of police bullets. In the background, there was a slow love song playing from a megaphone in one of the police vans. And then I died like a B-grade Hindi movie villain, slowly grudgingly, blood flowing from my seventeen bullet wounds viscously, reluctantly. The audience whistled and applauded my gruesome end.

There were cherry red bruises all over my reflection in the wash basin mirror.

I heard the apartment door shut quietly, the noise stealthy and reluctant. Maybe there was a reward for my capture now and the security guard had pocketed my five hundred bucks as well as called the police.

I craved alcohol.

I walked out gingerly to the living room and found Ogre, looking as mauled and bloodied as me, sitting on the bean bag, looking dazed.

"The police are on the lookout for me because of you! What have you been up to?" I almost shouted at him.

Ogre just stared at the floor, breathing heavily as if he had just run up the four flights of stairs to our flat.

"AND WHAT THE FUCK IS WRONG WITH YOUR GIRLFRIEND!" I shouted at him.

He finally looked at me and I saw that his face was bleeding. There was also a magnificent black circle around his right eye.

"What did you tell the police?" he asked quietly.

"Nothing!" I exclaimed. "What happened to you?"

"I am tired of this shit now," he said quietly.

And with that he turned his left hand at me as if to aim something at me.

The first thought I had was that Ogre's hand had turned to silver. And then I saw the gun.

It was a sparkling silver; it wasn't an automatic but one of those old fashioned ones that have a central rotating bullet housing cylinder.

The first bullet missed me by a couple of feet, thudding

gently into the bean bag.

"What the fuck!" I yelled.

The cylinder rotated majestically as the mechanism lined up another bullet for the gun to dispense.

"Don't worry," said Ogre calmly, "if I had meant to hit you, I would have."

His right leg shook restlessly and he had that menacing evil look in his eye that made him look like the B-grade Hindi movie villain he had been.

He continued quietly, "Here's what is wrong... you screwed up. And at the absolutely worst possible time."

"Screw up what?" I asked, not sure whether still to be agitated or afraid.

Ogre held up his non-gun hand and showed me four fingers, "Four flawless plans and the police don't get one clue. And then you get on that investigation committee and they are on to us."

"Asshole! You know I didn't tell those guys anything!" I reacted.

"How am I to know?" Ogre retorted, pointing his gun barrel nonchalantly at me. Ogre, the picture perfect B-grade movie villain.

I began moving slowly towards the door. His gun hand followed.

"Because we're best friends and I would never screw you over, would I?" I said simply, hoping he would believe me.

Ogre sighed. "The final plan is bigger than you and me... bigger than our friendship. And I just can't take any more chances."

And with that Ogre levelled the gun at me and fired.

∞

We were bored, I remembered. Completely bored and suffocated in that farce of a party.

"Want to see something cool?" Ryan asked.

I nodded.

He pulled out something that looked like a tablet from his pocket and dropped it into one of the champagne glasses a passing waiter was carrying.

Nothing happened.

"Wait for it," he said.

I sipped from my glass quietly, disappointed.

"There," he said pointing.

Nothing happened for a millisecond.

A millisecond later, champagne burst up from the glass like lava from a volcano causing the distracted waiter to drop the entire tray. One of the three Swatis I had met screamed like a banshee.

Swati had been a rather popular name in my generation. If I had a girl child I would have named her "Girl One" rather than inflict something like 'Swati' or 'Neha' or 'Richa' on her, a name so common that there would almost always be at least three of your kind wherever you went, screaming like a banshee to boot.

"Mentos and Carbon Dioxide... the most basic explosion you'll get," Ryan said pulling me away from my mental thesis on Swatikind.

I had known that, sort of, somewhere in the back of my head.

Ogre knew a lot of useless stuff. He told me that the best poison was antifreeze; it tasted sweet and was virtually impossible to detect in autopsies.

The best way to put someone in a deep sleep was to put pressure on their carotid artery for six seconds.

The best beer was a German brand I had not heard of.

I listened and nodded politely.

The best bomb was a cylinder of dry ice, for some reason.

The best music band ever was Eve6.

"Do you want to see something cool?"

I nodded.

Of course I did.

My mission and vision in life was to see something cool.

I followed Ogre out through a side exit. No one seemed to notice.

We walked for some time, down a long corridor, then up a couple of flights of stairs.

We reached what looked like the roof of ABCDEF Corp.'s office.

"That's where they keep the piss," Ogre said pointing out to a succession of large rubber tanks.

"What?" I exclaimed in surprise.

"You heard me right," he continued smiling. "One of the old timers told me."

I looked at the majestic giant rubber cylinders bewildered. What magnificent lunacy would drive someone to store piss in overhead tanks?

Ogre answered the confused expression on my face. "The company got fixated on doing this bio conservation thingy a couple of years ago. There's this European technology that can convert piss into some kind of bio fuel."

"So the company makes bio fuel from human urine?"

"Male urine only," he answered, as if the gender of the liquid was of utmost & critical importance. "The coolest thing is that the company that owned the proprietary technology and was putting the infrastructure in place was from Eastern Europe and went bankrupt in the last recession. So all they were able to do was to put in place this magnificent mechanism that transports male piss to the top of the building."

"So what happens to all the thingamajig stored here?" I asked.

"Nothing. At the end of every day one of the peons comes up here and twists a lever and all the piss flows down into sewage," Ogre concluded.

I felt my first ever pang of corporate regret. I had agreed to work for a firm which stored giant vats of piss on its roof.

"Imagine if one of these were to burst," Ogre said dreamily. "Piss would rain from the heavens."

A wave of disgust passed over me.

"That room in the corner is one of the company's data centres," Ogre said, pointing out towards a large locked air-conditioned room alongside the huge vats of piss.

My eyes were beginning to get tired and droopy from the drinking. I turned my weary eyeballs towards what Ogre was pointing out only for something flashy to catch my attention.

And at this point, I regained consciousness.

∞

There was a small round bullet shaped hole in my shirt collar. There was absolutely no blood however. I was almost disappointed.

There was no doubt in my mind that Ogre had shot to kill. The bullet had missed by no more than a centimetre; one centimetre to the right and it would have severed one of my critical arteries, my neck spraying blood like a leaky faucet. My own heartbeat would have pumped me to death.

It was almost embarrassing that I had fallen unconscious from the shock of seeing a bullet come at me. But it had also saved my life for Ogre had clearly presumed I had perished and left.

Reality was beginning to dawn on me painfully like sunlight does when you have a bad hangover. There were pieces of an idea forming in my head.

I craved alcohol.

I walked up to the fridge and gulped down one bottle of beer in ten seconds.

I put the empty bottle down and my brain activated almost instantly with the '*Clink*' sound of glass bottle meeting kitchen tile.

I knew what I was going to do next.

Insert coin to continue.

The Plan

There was no doubt in my mind that Ogre's girlfriend was a critical part of this jigsaw. Ira was the key to this puzzle. She knew something I didn't.

My mission and vision is to find Ira Sharma. Ira Sharma and her evil little red car from the most deeply regretted evil red memory of my life.

Her mobile was not reachable.

There were semblances of a plan forming in my head but I could only see what I had to do next.

A voice in my head said simply '*Run*'.

So I began to run. I ran out the house, down the four flights of stairs of our building, past the security guard and on to the cobbled street.

I craved alcohol.

The voice in my head continued. '*Run*' it said in a muted scream.

I ran like a madman, faster than I thought my limbs could have carried me. My head got clearer from the exercise, clear enough for me to understand in a momentary flash of brightness what my legs were taking me towards.

Bombay accepted the madness of my running as normalcy. Very few people stared; those who did did so with an uncanny unquestioning acceptance of the bizarre. I blended in and out of traffic; for most of the time I outpaced vehicles stuck in the highway's mad traffic.

I felt stronger, bigger, faster than I actually was, almost as big as Ogre. Running did not exhaust me; rather it seemed to power me. I had hardly ever felt such energy, such electricity running through my body. I felt powerful enough to take Ogre down with one punch and deflect his next bullet with my skin, suddenly bulletproof from all the running.

The large rusting metallic hoarding board that said "XYZ College" was pink in color. Pink like a sanitary napkin pack. Pinker than an indigestion tablet.

The girls' hostel was five kilometres down the road, someone told me. So I ran.

The voice in my head told me that that was where she was.

I felt Bombay's humidity rake up sweat on me. The back of my neck bristled and burned with millions of pearls of sweat, all adding their weight, attempting to slow me down. But I ran like a madman only mindful of one single burning flaming aim.

My mission and vision in life is to locate Ira Sharma.

I ran like a madman.

I ran and realized that my life was even cheaper than ABCDEF Corp.'s evaluation. I was 500 bucks per day to Prakash, the security guard. I was a bullet of 200 bucks for all my days to Ogre. I was a 5 buck coin of Ira Sharma's evil little red car game.

No amount of piss could liberate me.

I ran like a madman; turned left onto an empty road.

A mosquito whizzed past my left ear.

I ran, the madman in me incapable of being flustered by whizzing mosquitoes.

A second mosquito whizzed and thudded into just below my left shoulder blade with incredible force. My concentration broke and I staggered and fell.

I felt dizzy and dazed; my shoulder was rendered immobile. I watched my shadow take a distinct human shape beneath me as I lay sprawled on the ground.

I saw blood begin to fill out my shadow as if a crazier, much Darker Lord wanted to review my worthless pitiful existence with crayons and colour filling in shapes again.

I looked up and saw a human figure looking down at me, his head coming at me from the sun, a shiny silver gun in his left hand.

Most people go through their entire lives without ever fully understanding how a bullet works. That, of course, is a tremendous shame.

A gun is the perfect manifestation of the age old human

instinct to kill. You pull the trigger and in the split second in which you'll have your intended target sprawled on the ground – his blood filling out into his shadow like a bad mid-year appraisal – several small little things happen that you (being 'most people') will never have the slightest inkling of.

Once you have pulled it, the trigger works like a piston that pushes the bullet into the barrel and sets fire to the gunpowder, an explosive chemical that will push the bullet out of the barrel with the enormous amount of heat and gases generated by its burning.

Ogre once told me that the most gruesome way to kill someone was to replace the nicotine in their cigarette with gunpowder. That would make for an excellent anti smoking campaign, filling up one cigarette in hundred with gunpowder.

I only knew this because Ogre knew this.

The man from the sun who had shot me looked down at me like a villainous demi-god. He was clearly in no hurry to finish me off.

And that was my last sane thought as I passed out for the third time in the day.

∞

I became an asteroid again. Only the planets this time were much less bouncier.

From my semi-conscious realm, I felt I was in a vehicle with agitated confused voices around me. I caught snatches of conversation around me that I did not comprehend. Or I absorbed sub-consciously but did not understand.

My vision began to flicker on for a few seconds at a time. I saw that my shirt was drenched with blood in one flash.

The next flash put a face in my head, a male bearded face that was familiar but I could not recognize.

I felt a vicious stab in my shoulder and my brain blanked out from the pain. I did not return to earth for a couple of minutes.

The next flash of consciousness told me that there was a woman driving the vehicle. A woman who looked much older than me.

My last thought as I passed out for good was that the woman could describe every producer and casting director in the city in bed. Vividly.

When I came to next, I found myself in a bed, not mine, a slowly whirring fan pouring down waves of welcome cool on me. There was moonlight coming in through a window to my right.

I could not move my shoulder; it seemed to be made of stone. I saw that it was bandaged.

With an almost almighty effort, I got out of bed and walked towards the moonlight.

I saw that I was directly opposite ABCDEF Corp.'s building.

And there winking at me mischievously was the magical beauty of my dreams.

Endgame

Those Basilisk eyes frolicked, laughed, spun, danced, committed mischiefs. They mocked my wonder, stared at me with quiet disdain.

"She's quite something, isn't she?"

Shocked by the sudden noise, I jerked my head back suddenly towards the source of it and pulled a muscle in the shoulder that had been shot, causing a ten second sensory blackout.

I returned from the pain orbit to find Ogre sitting in a chair staring at me with laughing eyes.

"You have to say she looks a lot different now. This picture was taken almost three years ago," Ogre continued, his tone macabre and scary as a bleeding bullet wound. "I am not surprised you did not recognize her. Even I didn't, for some time. This was the time she was trying to become Miss India."

I turned to face him. Moonlight lit his face up but the rest of him remained in darkness; I had no clue if he was still carrying his gun.

My mission and vision is to not get shot again.

"Who are you talking about?" I asked, in a scared voice that was almost a whisper.

Ogre stood up and walked up to me slowly, his hands behind his back. He reached me and turned me around by my unwounded shoulder, back towards the memory that had been haunting me for what seemed like ages.

Trapped in a time warp – in an old fraying hoarding atop the building adjacent to our office, not more than ten feet away from the vats of piss atop our office building – was the woman of my dreams. The best part about the hoarding was that it wasn't visible at all from the road below, but only from the higher floors of the buildings opposite or from the roof of ABCDEF Corp. itself.

Our doe eyed beauty was extolling a skin whitening/ fair complexion inducing brand that had most likely long died in the country. Beneath the divine face of the magical beauty from my memory was written a tagline that had clearly been idiotproofed: *makes skin whiter.*

Face White.

Makes skin whiter.

Period.

No other mission or vision in life.

One edge of the hoarding which contained her divine Majesty's hair had come off its hinges from age and the wind played merrily with it. Moonlight and a couple of flickering streetlights cast oblique illumination on her, making her eyes look magical, making them dance, frolic, rake up happy memories.

Her divinity was nothing but an optical illusion.

I craved alcohol.

Ogre grinned at me like a madman. "She's quite something, isn't she?" he repeated.

And then I saw her again. Her eyes evil and undivine without the flickering light, her hair human without the wind playing with them, I saw her to be who she actually was. An evil menacing witch.

"Too bad we broke up," Ogre said quietly, in a voice laced with mischief.

I looked at Ira Sharma of three years ago, Ira Sharma of the part time model, the Miss India aspirant and the hauntingly beautiful damnably evil memory I had somehow suppressed for a long time. She stared back at me with evil unsmiling, ungrateful eyes. Eyes so evil and poisonous that it was no wonder the damn brand died.

There was a voice playing over and over again in my head. *That woman of your dreams, those eyes that have been haunting you all this time belonged to Ira Sharma.*

Jesus H Christ, you're screwed!

"You do understand there is something wrong with this picture, don't you?" Ogre asked me.

I stared at the hoarding with renewed interest and a split second later instinctively understood he was not referring to it.

"Back up to the night you blew up RK's car," he said, a malicious grin beginning to form on his face.

"I did not!" I exclaimed.

"Of course you did," Ogre quipped. "But your placement can at best be described as amateurish. The car almost didn't blow up."

I stared at the hoarding in silence, unsure of how to respond to Ogre's allegation.

He patted me on the uninjured shoulder, "But I'm still proud of you. Excellent use of dry ice."

I looked at him, confused. Paragraphs from my chemical engineering bible fluttered in front of my eyes. *Dry ice or solidified Carbon Dioxide, apart from its uses in refrigeration, has increasingly come to be used as an explosive device. Terrorist and criminal groups place dry ice in a container sealed tight...*

"...generally with some amount of water in it," Ogre took over from the Jain & Jain text in my head. "In the ensuing heat transfer between water and the extremely cold solid, dry ice begins to sublimate to Carbon Dioxide inside the container thereby building pressure inside the sealed container."

Ogre grinned from ear to ear like the Cheshire Cat.

"Finally the container cannot withstand the pressure and it bursts," he continued. "In other words, boom!"

I turned to face my best friend and archenemy. "Why did you blow up RK's car?" I asked, exasperated.

The Cheshire Cat grin was so wide that Ogre could not speak for a minute.

"I learnt, of course, that the explosion was not satisfying at all," Ogre continued without answering. "The problem was that as soon as the glass shards penetrated the CNG cylinder, the gas exploded almost instantly causing the entire dry ice mass to turn to Carbon Dioxide in a microsecond. And Carbon Dioxide as you know is famously used for extinguishing fires. The blast lasted barely a couple of seconds." His face was marked with regret.

In the distance, I could hear the wailing sirens of an ambulance.

"The significantly more important question is do you understand what is wrong with this picture?"

The ambulance siren was louder, almost as if it was in my head.

"You blew up RK's car as a trial for something bigger that you... your people are planning?"

Ogre frowned as he mulled my answer over. "I'll give you that one. Not the one I was looking for again though."

The ambulance siren was in my head now. I looked down from the window and saw a white Maruti van with the name of an obscure hospital written on it stop in front of our building.

"It was you who shot me? Because you thought I had betrayed you?" I asked.

"I did shoot you, yes," Ogre said without revealing his motive.

The back doors of the ambulance opened and someone was dragged out of it, kicking and screaming, by a couple of men who looked oddly familiar.

I looked away and saw that Ogre was almost in my face. "The right question to ask is, my friend, what is your name?"

The Adventures of Ryan

I searched myself as if I were searching for a pen. My brain returned a database error.

I did not have a name.

I was Ravi SuperAwesome Prasad, amongst other names. I played the guitar and loved working out.

I saw that the kicking and screaming being was bound and gagged and was giving the two oddly familiar goons a tough time as they tried to maneuver it.

I had many names. I was Kunal who was a footballer and loved to write poetry. Then, I was Puneet who was a nerd hooked on Alistair Maclean novels.

I knew what Ogre's final move was going to be but I did not know my name. It was lost in one of the many pockets of my mind.

As far back as I could think, I did not have a recollection of having a name. I craved alcohol.

Outside, the night was a dark humid macabre Bombay night, hanging droopily on all that exists. There was an ominous stillness in the air, as if even the dark was aware of the impending death and destruction. The two goons had successfully managed to usher the screaming, kicking, bound, gagged being into our building.

Ogre opened his mouth to speak and finally said what I was dreading would be the truth. "Your name is Ryan Mascarenhas."

There was a blinding pain in my head as bad as the bullet wound in my shoulder. Ira Sharma of the hoarding looked at me with her usual evil contempt.

I had searched all my mental pockets for it and not found it on me.

"Do you remember the first time you met me?" Ogre asked.

"I was wearing your tag," I said sheepishly.

Ogre laughed his villainous laugh. "And you were dead drunk."

"That *was* my tag… My name *is* Ryan Mascarenhas, isn't it?" I asked.

Ogre smiled at me and nodded.

"And that's the whole picture, isn't it?" I said. "You've never really existed."

There was a wall of silence in the room between us. It was as if I was speaking to myself from a distance.

"Cut back to when you first met me at that induction party," Ogre said looking somehow more menacing than he ever had. "You were drunk and forlorn and lonely. You have always had an inherent inability to make friends anyway."

It was clear now why I knew what Ogre was going to do tonight.

We shared the same brain. Always had.

"And then you conjured me up," Ogre continued. "You thought I was the night's entertainment, didn't you? Too bad, I stayed…"

I looked out of the window in silence. I was a character stuck in a Palahnuik book, a six foot tall monster that had to come to call itself Ogre. As I stood a couple of feet from him, it was hard to know which one of us was real and which imagination.

"The beer that we've been having… well you've been having… why do you think it's so expensive?" Ogre said. "It has certain tryptamines which are…"

"…hallucinogens," I completed Ogre's sentence.

Hallucinogens. Drugs that induce hallucinations.

Jain & Jain Chapter Twelve.

Ogre knew this because I knew this. Or vice versa.

It didn't really matter.

Now I knew why I craved alcohol so much. Without our expensive drug-laced beer, I had withdrawal symptoms.

It all made sense now.

I did blow up RK's car though I had no memory of it. I started a cult whose biggest act was going to happen tonight.

I wooed and broke up with Ira Sharma, the evil beauty of my dreams.

It was me all through. I was an alcohol and hallucinogen induced monster I had befriended.

Was I awake? Had I slept?

My mission is to collate my history.

I struggled in Bollywood for two years and did bit roles in films. I pissed in a famous Bollywood starlet's juice. I was a villainous expert at raping and murdering. And then I fell back and became an employee at a software firm that called itself, unimaginatively, 'ABCDEF Corp.' and eventually a B-school wannabe.

For some time now, I had been both Ogre and myself; I did not know I was which when.

I had no memory of doing any of the things Ogre had done. Except for the fact that he was a figment of my imagination, there was nothing to say that he wasn't a completely different being.

I craved alcohol.

"But why would I shoot myself?" I asked.

Far in the distance, I heard panting and grunting and shuffling of feet.

"Because, my friend," Ogre said simply "We needed to hijack an ambulance."

"What... why?"

"Because the police have been on our trail for some time

now and we needed a mode of transport that no one would stop, especially with the siren on," Ogre said.

The door burst open suddenly. The two men from the ambulance carried in the kicking and screaming bound human they had dragged up. I recognized them both. They were my friends from a past life. Ogre's friends. Both of them strugglers.

They looked at Ogre and he nodded. One of them placed a firm hand on the jugular of the creature, whose face was completely hidden behind a black cloth (the kind with which they obscure the faces of men who are being hanged to death) and the muted screams and kicking stopped. Carotid artery for six seconds.

The men then turned around and walked away in silence, still breathing a little heavily.

"You have figured out what I am going to do next, haven't you?" Ogre said. "The ice packs…"

"…gave you the Ammonium Nitrate you needed," I finished his sentence.

Ogre smiled and reached out for my shoulder wound and said, "You know too much." As he pressed onto my wound and I began to slide into darkness, I realized sheepishly that I was doing this to myself.

As my vision began to fade from the pain and I collapsed to the ground, I heard Ogre say, "My name is Ryan Mascarenhas. And I don't need you to drink to be Ryan anymore."

The Roof

Iregained consciousness to find my limbs bound to a wooden chair.

I saw that we were not in the room we had been anymore… there was no roof above us and the moon bathed us with its pale pathetic light. We were on the roof of the same building we had been in.

With moonlight as his aura, Ogre stood facing me like a messenger of death. The moonlight accentuated the bruises and red patches on his (and my) skin, clearly the side effects of handling ammonium nitrate.

Was I asleep? How long had I been dreaming?

Also bound to a wooden chair and with the black cloth of death-by-hanging now removed was an unconscious Ira Sharma. I did not know why Ogre had arranged for her to be here.

Ogre looked at me and began to speak.

"Before there were pistols," Ogre said, "killing people with a bullet was a tedious task."

He flashed me this smile as if all this were merely a secret joke between friends.

"An average musket weighed about three odd kilograms, more than twice the weight of today's automatics. You began with taking the musket in your hand and holding it parallel to your body, its butt resting on the ground. Then you took this paper pouch out of your pocket and tore its seal off with your teeth, invariably ingesting some of the gunpowder meant for your musket."

Ogre circled around us, scratching his forehead with his finger, his gun trained at me all through.

"You then poured the gunpowder down your musket's throat and waited a split second for it to settle in. You followed this up by turning to one of your other pockets, the one that contained the bullets."

He came to a momentary stop behind me. "The first bullets were round and made of lead. The US Civil War spawned an entire cottage industry of round lead bullet makers."

Ogre came around to face me and looked sadly at the pistol in his hand. "They don't make that anymore, those flawed homemade round lead pellets," he said nostalgically. "Everything is about precision and science these days." He shook his head sadly.

Ira Sharma of the decayed hoarding opposite us looked at me omnisciently.

As Ogre went on about the beauty of the gun, I realized

that the streets were completely empty; there were no sounds whatsoever. It meant that it was probably around or beyond midnight. Bombay was asleep.

"Just imagine yourself as a soldier two hundred years ago," Ogre said. "If the enemy came at you shooting, you would have to stand sheepishly going through the entire twenty second process of cleaning your barrel, opening your bullet sack and fixing in the bullet and gunpowder. Just imagine the horror of knowing that your life, in those twenty seconds, was in the hands of someone else."

I tried desperately to keep the plan forming in my head from reaching Ogre, invoking all my mental strength or whatever was left of it.

Ogre now sat on his haunches in front of us – me, semi conscious and struggling to collect his wits for a last ditch desperate attempt for his life, and the evil demoness Ira Sharma, unconscious as a patient in a coma.

"What you do not understand, Ryan," Ogre said, his voice betraying a finality as if we were close to the end of our story, "is that if in your twenty seconds you had embraced the possibility of impending death instead of cleaning the barrel vigorously, you won't ever have needed me."

I began struggling against the bonds on my hands. Both my arms were behind the chair, tied to the rear leg of the wooden chair. It struck me how odd my situation was, bound, held captive and about to be killed off by a figment of my own imagination.

"But you struggled and flailed, and never really gave in to the thought that maybe your life was never going to be a success… maybe your name was written on that enemy bullet," he said bitterly. "You just focused on the one thing you saw, your gun barrel, and never saw the bullet with your death on it coming."

The bonds were tight enough to make my struggle futile. I had no clue how I had managed to do that to myself.

"Not to say that you haven't been an immense help to me," Ogre continued, standing up, beginning to turn away from me. To my side, I heard Ira breathing heavily in her coma. "I couldn't have done any of this without your knowledge of chemistry or programming. Your life, my friend, has not been completely in vain."

And with that, he turned completely bringing himself to face Ira Sharma of the hoarding and our office building.

"And FYI," he said, "Pay-Day went live today. I would put that on my CV if I were you. But then I *am* you." I imagined him smirking.

Were my hands really tied behind my back? How the hell had I managed to do that?

I saw Ogre raise his gun hand slowly towards the damn beauty trapped in the hoarding, slowly like a professional murderer and rapist and villain. I realized it was already too late to try and untie myself.

"Goodbye and good night, folks!" Ogre said cheerily. "It's been one hell of a ride!"

He began to take aim. I got up on my feet, keeping my back at the angle of the chair tied to me and began to run at him like a raging bull carrying a chair on its back. Ogre fired.

In the two seconds before I hit him, several things happened quickly. The trigger set light to the gunpowder which in turn exploded causing one fateful bullet to scream out of the barrel at about a thousand kilometres per hour. The bullet in turn whizzed towards Ogre's intended target while I was still about one-and-a-half seconds away from him. In the one second before I hit Ogre, the bullet penetrated the metallic skull of the cylinder it hit at a speed in the high hundreds of kilometres per hour (with the wind en route shaving off some of the bullet's speed) causing the metal at the site of impact to ignite and give rise to a few sparks. The sparks in turn caused oxygen contained inside this cylinder to explode ferociously, setting off a chain reaction of cylinders exploding.

I hit Ogre at the point of the explosion getting to the ammonium nitrate bomb Ogre had placed on the roof of ABCDEF Corp.'s office (in addition to the cylinders most likely taken from the ambulance). I felt the surprise in the way his body reacted. He had not expected a fight in me.

As I crashed into Ogre with his body giving in meekly to my force, the fire reached the ammonium nitrate from the ice packs stored previously in our house.

We reached the precipice of the roof in a millisecond –

us, the raging bull and its villainous victim – and began the fall down to the ground that I was sure would kill Ogre. I felt sure that, as in the cartoons, I would land on Ogre and survive the fall. Which was, of course, a ridiculous idea.

And then as we were in the first millisecond of the fall downward and I could imagine the look of shock and horror on Ogre's face, the explosion got nuclear. The ammonium nitrate bomb on the roof opposite ignited and set off a shockwave that for one split second, arrested our fall and in the next evil explosive split second, sent both of us flying back on to the roof, away from the clutches of gravity, back on to Ogre's territory.

We went flying over Ira's chair and landed ten feet behind her. We landed Tom & Jerry like in a crash – Ogre's over six feet tall huge frame crashing into me like a delicious afterthought of the explosion. I felt the chair's wooden limbs impale me and Ogre's impact on top of me crack most of my ribs.

I looked above at the dead skies of Bombay trying to locate something, anything that I could hang on to in my vicious pain. But I saw nothing... only pollution obscured darkness.

I saw one of the wooden legs of the chair stick out at an odd angle from somewhere on my body and knew this was the end.

In a pain inspired flash, I saw the skull on the back of the beer bottle above me in the sky, possibly warning me in some unintelligible language that drinking would eventually cause my death.

I screamed for help and found my cries lost in the cackle of the fire and mini explosions still rankling through the ABCDEF Corp. office building. My last living memory was that it had begun to rain.

And then I died.

Epilogue

Thirty minutes later, I woke up when I heard someone whispering my name.

I opened my eyes and saw the face of the woman of my dreams. She cradled me and whispered again softly, "Wake up, Ryan!"

I could hear it raining in the distance but the sky above me was completely dry.

I woke up with a clear painless head. I had scratches and burns yes, but all my fatal wounds were gone.

Ira stopped whispering when she saw me open my eyes. She just looked at me with her big magical mesmerizing Basilisk eyes, wide with fear.

There *was* a part of me that had died with my fatal wounds. I sat up feeling as if nothing had happened, feeling stronger, faster, bigger.

I woke up as Ogre.

My imagination had become me. I was long dead.

I/Ogre stood up gingerly and looked at the scene in

front of me with wonder. The entire plan had gone down perfectly. In the distance, I heard the wails of several sirens.

Not many people knew or would ever know that it was I who had leaked those fudged financials – I had come across while making RK's deck – to the media. I had destroyed ABCDEF Corp. long before my explosion had destroyed it.

I couldn't resist raising my arms to the heavens in victory. There was still a bullet hole in my shoulder but I felt very little pain. Ryan, the MBA aspirant, had died taking all my pain with him. I was Ogre, Ryan's monster, villainous rapist and murderer, basking in my success, no more a mere mediocre henchman.

In front of me, the building burnt satisfactorily. If you worked at ABCDEF Corp., you would be forced to take a leave today because your office was burning satisfactorily to the ground. Which was a good thing because you were only allowed two weeks of casual leave per year and 180 days of sick leave all through your life. Which effectively meant that over a forty year career, you were only allowed to fall sick four-and-a-half days per year. Any more than that and they would cut your salary.

And it all burnt in front of me: all those leave records, all those records of employee appraisals, all those mindless layers of code that did nothing but make money for a company that paid you nowhere close to enough for the abject torture your work was and then made away with your annual bonus without so much as an apology.

The bomb had been placed strategically atop the data centre on the roof and the room had been totally annihilated, completely destroying every bit of data in it. The hoarding with my beauty of three years ago was magically intact, except for its underside which had turned a merry red. Most of the vats of piss were gone and a couple of them were disfigured and sprouting the liquid they held.

Piss rained from the heavens.

I smiled.

I realized Ira was standing beside me staring wide-eyed at the burning building. I held her hand without saying anything. She did not say a word either.

We just stared at the scene in front of us like an odd couple belonging to a species borne of destruction.

When the explosion had occurred, aside from the added unexpected bonus of killing the weak and ineffective side of my brain, it became the final cog in the wheels of my revenge. As Pay-Day had been pilot-launched the day before, ABCDEF Corp. had become the first company to adopt the system for itself. And as the fire cackled, merrily eating away all digital employee records the data centre held, salaries had begun to be credited to employee accounts. What nobody knew and would not know for some time was that Sudeep and I had planted a virus that would allocate the salary pool only amongst those who had lost their bonuses in the company stock, were we ever to lose contact with the data centre.

There would be no salary paid out to the CXOs, none to the Board, none to anybody who hadn't lost what we had lost.

All they would get was fire and ash.

Ira looked at me and asked in a small voice, "Wh… what happened here?"

Of course they would correct the error soon, I thought. In a fortnight, maybe even a week. But by then we would have already made a deep cut on their psyche. We would have showed them that slaves we might be, but we still had a fight in us.

I, for one, had plans to transfer the money out of my salary account and out of the country within the next hour. As the leader of the cult, I took the CEO's salary, which was ten times the money I had made till now in my four years of slavery. Maybe I would run away to a foreign country. Nepal? Dubai?

"What are you thinking?" Ira said, looking at me with her big scared eyes.

I remembered that there was a reason why I had gotten her here.

"Hi," I said.

She looked confused for a second. And then replied, "Hi."

"I *am* an asshole," I said, smiling. In front of us the building was now beginning to creak, burnt bits and pieces of it falling to the ground.

"And I am sorry for that."

She just stared at me wide eyed and confused.

"Ira Sharma, I met you at a very strange time in my life," I said, pulling her towards me.

I moved my face towards her and closed my eyes, like a deranged tire mechanic. She gave in without protest and as we kissed, the building came down behind us with an almighty explosion.

A very satisfying explosion.

I let go but she hugged me and as she burrowed her head into my shoulder, I could feel a smile form on her lips. A moment of pure magic passed between us; us – skin to skin holding each other tight.

Ira Sharma.

The magical beauty of my dreams.